The Secrets of Cranberry Beach

Case No. 2

A Belltown Mystery

By
T. M. Murphy

J. N. TOWNSEND PUBLISHING
EXETER, NEW HAMPSHIRE
2001

Cover illustration © 2001. Mark Penta.
Printed in Canada
Published by J. N. Townsend Publishing
   12 Greenleaf Drive
   Exeter, NH 03833
   603/778-9883
   800/333-9883
   www.jntownsendpublishing.com
   www.belltownmysteries.com
Cataloging-in-Publication Data
Murphy, Ted, 1969-
   The secrets of Cranberry Beach / by T.M. Murphy.
   p. cm. – (A Belltown mystery ; no. 2)
   Summary: Teen detective Orville Jacques confronts dangerous killers while trying to solve a number of crimes that have stymied investigators in his Cape Cod town for forty years.
   [1. Mystery and detective stories. 2. High schools—Fiction. 3. Schools—Fiction. 4. Cape Cod (Mass.)—Fiction.] I. Title.
   PZ7.M9565 Sg 2001
   [Fic]—dc21   2001035152

2nd Printing

1-880158-36-1

Thanks to Mark Penta, Cheeka,

the Harding, Stack, and Keating families

for all their support!

Special thanks to Mom & Dad for

encouraging me to make my own journey.

In Loving Memory of Jenny Chance

and Rick Robertson:

Young smiles that will not fade

with time, but will shine brightly

through eternity . . .

Acknowledgments

I would like to thank Rob Dube, Pat Pennucci, Betty Collins, Kay Lockhart, Sandy Mitchell, Tracey Frohock, Alanne Dugar, Maureen Devlin, Beth Melican, Tim Strazzere, John Forcucci, Marsha Malone, Greg Papsadora, Sean McEvoy, and Janet Valley for all their help with making the Belltown Mystery Series known to kids all over the world.

We all have friends, but true friends are people who stick by you when life isn't always going your way. I am blessed to call the following people my true friends: Sean Keating, Mark Penta, Dave Stack, Jay Oliveira, Andrea and Ethan Harding, Ed Murphy, Dennis Gilligan, Sarah Vallely, Mat Curran, Brian Connolly, Cheeka, Charlie Coté, Craig and Kenny Kozens, Scott Etler, Joe Crowley, Jackie McEvoy, Derrick Nelson, and Steve and Paula Kapulka.

CHAPTER ONE

I HATED IT! I mean I hated every bit of it. I don't want to sound like one of those people who is suddenly thrust into the limelight and refuses to drive in the limo, since I didn't refuse the limo ride before the governor's citizens' awards dinner. In fact, I shouldn't say I hated *every* bit of it because I did love the limo ride, and I loved the fact that my date was Kim Archer, a senior and head cheerleader. It was pretty awesome sitting in the back of the long black stretch limo sipping an ice-cold soda and hearing the driver call me "sir." Me, sixteen-year-old Orville Jacques, was being called "sir."

"Sir. I hear you are a Red Sox fan. Would you and your date like me to drive by Fenway Park? We have half an hour before we have to be at Copley Plaza for the dinner."

"Yeah I'd love to see the CITGO sign all lit up," I said automatically.

The driver chuckled and put his foot on the gas, and we weaved in and out of traffic.

"Yeah, that sounds like real fun." Kim folded her arms and rolled her eyes.

"I'm sorry, did you want to go someplace else?"

"No, no. Fenway is so romantic." Her tone was sarcastic. I wanted to argue, but I kept quiet. I was quickly learning who Kim Archer was. She was no Maria Simpkins. I was going to ask Maria, the sweetest girl in Belltown, and also the girl of my dreams, but my friends told me I should make her jealous. That way, when I did ask her out she'd jump at the chance.

As we came to a stoplight on Commonwealth Avenue, a group of college kids peered into the smoke-colored windows, probably wondering if someone famous was inside. If they only knew it was a junior in high school with the cheerleading captain. I guess I was pretty famous, but after the governor's citizens' awards dinner I figured my fifteen minutes of fame would eventually run out. You see, I was going to receive a big-time medal or award or something from the governor. In August, I had solved a multiple-murder mystery, and I helped catch the killers. It was now mid-October, and the *Boston Globe* and the *Boston Herald* were still writing about it like I was one of the Hardy boys or something. That's what I hated! People loved how a sixteen-year-old kid stumbled onto a murder mystery, but, like anything, it gets old. I honestly couldn't wait to get back to my quiet autumn down on Belltown, Cape Cod.

We rolled past Fenway Park. It was dark except for the blue and red lights on the CITGO sign that sent the message that Fenway wasn't dead; it was just in a deep sleep until spring. After a few moments, the driver stepped on the gas, and we bombed away toward Copley Plaza.

"That was fun." Kim kept up her sarcasm while checking her makeup in her compact. I knew Maria would have enjoyed the moment, being a softball player, and now I was certain I had made a mistake.

"So, sir. Are you ready for your big night?" The driver looked straight ahead.

"I'm, ah, could you just call me, Orville. And this is Kim."

"Oh, sure, Orville and Kim. Good to meet you. I'm Ryan."

"Good to meet you, Ryan." I put my hand over the seat and Ryan shook it, keeping the other hand on the wheel. Kim just grunted as she touched up her nails with red polish. "To answer your question, I'm definitely honored, but I'm kind of sick of all the attention. I've had to wear a tie almost every day. I hate ties. I can't even tie ties. And the media ..."

"Yeah, they've written a lot about you."

"You'd think I had won the Heisman Trophy." Ryan and I laughed.

"You see Orville, with all the negative stuff going on in the world, your story is pretty refreshing."

I smiled. That did make me feel good.

"Well, get ready, guys. Here we are." He put on the turn signal. We pulled up in front of Copley Plaza, and there were about a dozen reporters waiting outside the limo. Bright lights, TV cameras, microphones, the whole nine yards.

"Now I know why my parents decided to drive to this thing. Well, it was nice meeting you, Ryan."

"It was nice meeting you both." He tried including Kim, but she was too busy smiling out the window.

"Orville, I'll get the door." Ryan jumped out of the limo, walked over and opened the door to the tunnel of bright lights.

"Orville, here's my card. If you're ever in Boston and need free transportation or anything, call me." He shook my hand.

"I can't . . ."

"Yes, you can. You did a great thing." He smiled.

"Thanks." I turned toward the bright lights and then whispered back, "In a week I'll be out like the seventies."

"Hey, who says they're out? That was my generation." Ryan smiled.

I laughed and approached the chorus of, "Orville, Orville . . ."

There were about a hundred and fifty people at the

dinner ceremony. Kim and I met up with my family, and for a half hour everyone walked around and socialized. I met all sorts of people. The governor was pretty down to earth, and the president of the Senate had a great sense of humor. It was exciting talking to the police detectives because they really appreciated my investigative work. The only bad part was while I was doing all the talking, the trays of hors d' oeuvres were passing by me, and my brother Billy and sister Jackie and Kim were doing all the eating. I mean, it's pretty rude to tell the governor of Massachusetts, "Hold on a minute, I gotta get one of those scallops wrapped in bacon."

My stomach was making those embarrassing growling noises, the kind that only seem to happen whenever you're taking a history test. Finally, we got to sit down at the head table with the governor, the other four recipients, and their families. All the other recipients had saved lives. There was a seven-year-old girl who saved her brother from choking; a twenty-year-old guy who saved a man from getting mugged; a forty-year-old woman cashier who hit a would-be-robber over the head with a bottle of Dom Perignon champagne; a seventy-six-year-old woman who had pulled a boy out of a pond after he fell through the ice; and me. We were quite the motley crew.

When the food came, I devoured prime rib and potatoes and a huge slice of fancy ice-cream cake. I was feeling pretty good until the governor got up on the stage by our table.

"Ladies and gentlemen. We are here to celebrate five people who range in age from seven to seventy-six."

The governor said a few more words about us and motioned to our table, and everyone gave us a standing ovation. We were all visibly embarrassed. I was nervous. I don't know why I felt that way. It wasn't as though I had to give a speech or anything.

When the applause died down and everyone got back into their seats, the governor continued. He introduced Tyrone Jackson, the twenty-year-old who'd saved the man who was being mugged. The governor told how, while Tyrone was walking home from the library where he went to college, he saw the crime taking place.

He threw his backpack, knocking one of the assailants down, and then took on the other one until the police were able to come to the scene. The governor concluded, "Tyrone, would you come up here and say a few words?"

Tyrone looked over at me, and I knew he was shocked that he had to speak. In fact, the whole table was in shock, and now I knew why I was nervous. Tyrone approached the podium, and once he began I could tell the mike was his friend.

"Guess, I want to say I'm very honored to accept this award, and I want to thank my parents for raising me to know right from wrong and to act when I see wrong. But, most of all, I would like to thank Professor Daniels. If he didn't make us buy all those heavy law books, I probably wouldn't have been able to knock the guy down with my backpack." The place erupted with laughter.

I wasn't laughing. I was trying to think of what I

could say. I kept searching my brain as the governor kept bringing up the honorees, one by one, and they all had a funny comment like the cashier who knocked the guy out with the bottle of Dom Perignon. "The only thing I regret is I didn't hit him with a bottle of the cheaper stuff. His head wasn't worth the Dom Perignon."

"The last recipient showed his heroism in somewhat of a different way. It was a little more than 'heat of the moment' heroics. In a few months of investigating this past summer, he was able to solve tragic and previously unknown multiple murders. Would Orville Jacques please come to the podium and say a few words?"

My parents were beaming as everyone gave me a huge hand. Everyone was expecting me to say something spectacular. My tongue was tied in a thousand knots as I went to the mike.

"I, ah, ah, just want to ah, a-h . . . I heard my own voice and my brain was saying could you say 'ah' one more time?

"Ah." I guess I could.

"I . . . ah want to thank my parents, of course. The governor. Y'know." I'm sounding like a loser, I thought. Who helped me on the case? I finally got control. "What I really want to say is it is really hard for me to celebrate this award because the reason I'm getting it is because people died, and we all assumed they died of natural causes. We now know that they didn't. So what I'm saying, is I'm honored but at the same time I'm sad. I hope in the future we will keep our eyes open. I do want to thank Detective Shane O'Connell of the Belltown police department and former detective Will Michaels for helping me and most of all believing me. Thank you." The governor put the medal around my neck and the applause came again.

The governor returned to the podium and said, "As for my parting words, I think Orville Jacques just put it into perspective. It is a shame we have to celebrate courage when it comes to robberies and murders. But, in celebrating the courage, it does show that there are good people in this state, and they are everyday people. And that means we all have the potential to do something special in our own lives. Thank you all and good night."

The final ovation came as the governor walked off the stage shaking hands. My parents hugged me as Kim and my brother and sister looked on. I was sweating and had to cool off, so I told them I had to go to the bathroom and that I'd meet them in the lobby. I made my way through the crowd saying, "Thank you" and nodding and stopping for a quick chat with well-wishers. When I got into the bathroom, I turned on the faucet and splashed water on my face. I didn't understand why I had been so nervous. It's not like I've never been in front of a crowd. I mean, I've been in a ton of plays, and I've been up with the winning run on base. This feeling was different. I hadn't been acting or playing. I was being me, and I guess I was a little insecure about how people saw me. The water cooled my face, and I thought, Hey, after the first few awkward seconds, I did pretty well.

I looked into the mirror to fix my hair and saw there was a man standing behind me. He was an old, wrinkled man with snow-white hair and dark blue eyes. He looked me up and down, and I was feeling uneasy, so I turned to face him. I could tell he was one of the retired policemen or detectives because he was wearing his old shield—number 566—and medals. I figured they were big-time medals because only the big-time retirees were invited to the dinner.

"Hi, how're you doing?" I said to break the silence.

"Good. Can I get around you to wash my hands?"

"Oh, yeah, sure." I moved so he could get by, but it seemed like he wanted to talk to me. It was really strange, so I waited a couple of seconds, and then I finally figured my hunch was wrong and headed to the door. His voice stopped me.

"So, you're the kid who solved that murder case." He soaped down his hands and looked at me through the mirror.

"Yes, sir. That's me."

"And in your speech you said Will Michaels helped you?" He washed off his hands.

"Yeah, Will was a big help. I couldn't have done it without him. Why? You know Will?"

"Oh, yes, I know Will. I worked with Will a couple of times on cases back in the forties."

"Really?" I couldn't believe it. Will never talked about his days as a cop or any of his past. I was kind of psyched that this man could tell me about my mentor.

"Really." He began drying his hands with a paper towel.

"What kind of cop was he?"

"Will Michaels was a dirty cop," the man said point blank as he crumpled his paper towel and threw it into the wastebasket.

"What? What? What do you mean he was dirty?" The words stung me. I couldn't believe what I was hearing. The man looked at his clean hands and then at me.

"He wasn't clean." The man turned and walked to the door.

"Wait! Wait!" I yelled. The man didn't stop as he opened the door. With that, my brother, Billy, came into the bathroom.

"Mom and Dad said to hurry up."

"Yeah, wait one second, I gotta find that guy." I stormed past Billy and opened the door, and the governor was standing right in front of me.

"Orville, just the man I'm looking for."

"Oh, hi, Governor." I looked past him trying to find the old man. I couldn't see him.

"Orville," the governor said to get my attention.

"Yes, sir." I reluctantly gave him what he wanted.

"What I was saying was I would like to get a couple of more pictures of Tyrone and you and the rest of the group before you go."

"Oh, OK." I didn't understand why he needed more pictures, but then I realized it was an election year.

While my brother and sister slept in the back of our new station wagon, my parents were talking a mile a minute to Kim on the way home about all the big-time people they met. The one time in my life I should've been on top of the world, I felt lousy. I just couldn't believe what that man had said about Will. Will a dirty cop. No way! But, then again, what did I really know about Will Michaels. I knew nothing of his past except that he once was a police detective. I met him while I was investigating the murders. I met the guy when he was a patient in a mental hospital. I knew he was there for depression, but I never did find out the cause of the depression. But, he helped me. He became my friend. Who was this guy calling Will a dirty cop? Why would he tell me that? As we entered Belltown I realized I knew who Will Michaels was *now,* but I didn't know who he was then. The words "dirty cop" stayed with me, and I knew I had to find out who Will Michaels was or had been . . .

CHAPTER
TWO

A WEEK HAD passed since the governor's dinner, and life was getting back to normal. The one memory that lingered was two words: dirty cop. I told myself not to think about it when I went to see Will after school. This was not the day to think negatively about Will. You see, after years of living in a mental hospital, Will was going to have his own apartment. Dr. Harris, Will's doctor, felt that his depression had come down to a degree where he could live on his own. She did warn me that he still might have his bad days, but it would help just for me to be positive and stay in his life. That meant I had to handle this "dirty cop" issue with extreme care. I didn't want to mention the past and set him off.

My friend Gina went with me to the Bayside Mental Hospital. We took her pickup truck because I still didn't have my license. Gina was my only girl best friend. She loved wearing platform shoes and listening to disco. She was different to say the least, but that was why everyone loved her. She was her own person, and if you didn't like it, too bad.

"Orville, I just got the *Best of the Seventies.* Do you want to listen to it? It's got everything:The Village People, Barry White, Diana Ross ..."

"What do *you* think, Gina?"

"Oh, yeah, you like all that old eighties junk like The Replacements."

"The Replacements are junk? Don't get me going, Gina. Anyway, how can you say 'old?' What do you think the seventies are? Why do you like that seventies music, anyway?"

"Because the seventies was such a tacky period in American history, therefore, it is one of the most unique periods and it should not be forgotten. It should be celebrated. Anyway, it's groovy." Gina turned up the volume and The Village People's "YMCA" entertained us while we drove to the Bayside Mental Hospital. All I could do is laugh at the irony. We were driving to a mental hospital, and I felt Gina's musical taste qualified her as a patient!

When we walked into the lobby, Will was waiting with Dr. Harris. He was all packed and ready to go to his new home. I could see he was nervous and excited. He kept checking his pockets and bags, making sure he had everything. Dr. Harris was just as nervous and excited.

She had a pad of paper with suggestions for him, and each time she was about to give it to him, she'd think of something else and take it back and write down another suggestion. After we packed the truck, I knew I had to speed up the process because Will was beginning to feel a little hesitant.

"All righty, Will. I think we're ready to roll."

"I guess so. Well, I just ah … want … " He turned to Dr. Harris and she wrapped her arms around him and gave him a hug and a kiss on the cheek.

"Will, you don't have to say anything. Now don't be so macho. Take your pills every day."

"Macho, macho man." Gina whispered in my ear, referring to another Village People song. I usually would have laughed, but I was really moved by how much Dr. Harris cared.

"Thank you." He hugged her and kissed her on the cheek.

All three of us packed into Gina's pickup and headed for Will's new apartment. Looking melancholic, Will stared at Bayside until it was out of view. Then he was his old self again.

"Gee, Orville and Gina, I've got to say, if I knew Dr. Harris fancied me that much I wouldn't have left." He let out a laugh and we joined in. Gina put her disco tape in and Will said, "Wow, I must've been in there a long time if disco's coming back."

We let out more laughter. I knew Will was beginning to feel comfortable. I tried to keep the laughter going by swapping jokes on the ride to Will's apartment. I didn't do this to make Will and Gina laugh. I did this to forget what was really on my mind—dirty cop.

Gina and I helped unload the truck and bring everything to Will's apartment, which was the downstairs of a two-family house. It was a comfortable, two-bedroom number that was completely furnished and overlooked Cranberry Beach. It's called Cranberry Beach because over a hundred years ago there was a hurricane, and the cranberries from the bogs up the street blew through the town, and thousands of them ended up on the beach. Well, at least that's what the townsfolk say.

"Will, you have to admit this view sure beats the view of the courtyard at Bayside. I mean, a lot of people would die to have a view of Cranberry Beach every day." Will put down one of his boxes and limped over to the window I was looking out.

"Orville, did you say Cranberry Beach?"

"Yeah, that's the name of the beach."

"I thought Dr. Harris was going to get me an apartment across from Sandy Point?" He looked concerned.

"Well, they call it Sandy Point now because of those condos on the point," I answered.

"Yeah, the developer named it Sandy Point, but most of the locals still call it Cranberry Beach," Gina added.

"Oh, my God," Will said softly as he stared at the beach.

"What's wrong, Will? Have you been to Cranberry Beach before? Is there something wrong with it?"

"No. No. It just reminds me of a place I once knew," Will insisted. I knew he was lying. I could see it in his face, and there was no way he could hide it. So he turned from the window and tried to avoid it.

"All right, let's get unpacked." He tried desperately to fake enthusiasm, but it was a weak attempt and I knew it.

"Will, what's in this shoe box?" Gina was holding a brown shoe box.

"Don't touch that shoe box! Put it down! Do you hear me?" We both stared. It was not like him. It was violent.

"I mean, where do you want me to put it?" Gina said nervously and looked to me for help.

"Just put it down. I'll take care of it." His tone wasn't as loud but it still was harsh.

"Hey, calm down, Will. Gina's just trying to help."

Will shut his eyes for a second before he responded. "I'm ... I'm sorry I snapped at you, Gina. It's not you guys. It's just been a long day, and I guess I'm a little nervous about living on my own. It's been a long time since I have, and I guess my nerves are kind of getting to me. Really, sorry."

Will put his hand out, and Gina put the box on the bed and then took his hand in hers.

"Don't worry about it, Will. I remember when I had to go to camp. The first couple of days I was scared about being on my own. I kind of acted like a real pain-in-the-you-know what. It was just because I was nervous. You'll get over it. And then in a few days you'll laugh at how nervous you were.

That was one of Gina's best qualities—she didn't let Will's outburst bother her. He apologized, and she let it roll off her back. I, on the other hand, was upset because I didn't buy his story of being nervous. Maybe he was, but I thought that his cracking jokes in the truck meant he was ready to move on. His attitude changed when I mentioned Cranberry Beach and when Gina picked up the shoe box. Why? About twenty minutes later, we finished unpacking and said our good-byes.

As I lay in bed that night, I tried to put Will out of my mind and decided to think about one of my favorite subjects—Maria Simpkins. I listened to my friends' advice and took Kim Archer to the big dinner. My friends told me that would send a clear message to Maria. I didn't like to play games but as my friend Scotty Donovan put it, "You tell someone how you really feel and in the end you'll get burned." So I took Kim to the big dinner. I had a lousy time. There was no way I was going to let another day go by without asking Maria out. I knew she had criminology class ninth period, and I had it tenth period, which was the last period of the day. I figured I would ask her right after ninth period and that way, if she said no, at least I wouldn't have to spend the rest of the day in school rejected, embarrassed, and depressed. I had a plan and sleep then came easily.

I was uncharacteristically confident approaching the girl of my dreams after ninth period. She was wearing a black suit jacket with matching pants. I don't really know how to describe it, but it looked like something out of *Vogue* magazine. Her long dark hair was in a bun, and it accentuated her soft cheekbones. The closer I got the more beautiful she looked and the great confidence was quickly fading, but I still managed, "Hey, Maria. How was criminology?"

"Hi, Orville," she said with a bright smile. Oh, that smile. She could melt Alaska with that smile.

"Crim was pretty cool. There's a retired policeman who's guest lecturer today. You'll love him. Just get him talking about old crimes and he'll go on forever." She held her books close to her and tilted her head, and I hadn't heard a word she had said. She waited for my response.

"That's cool." I figured whatever she said must've been cool. "Maria, I was wondering." I paused. It wasn't a dramatic pause. I just couldn't speak.

"Yeah, Orville." She kept smiling.

Say it all in one breath, I thought to myself.

"I was wondering, do you want to go out sometime? Y'know, like a date?" I pointed to her and then me. Why'd I do that? I thought. As if she couldn't understand me.

"I'd love to go out with you, Orville."

"That's great." I jumped in, maybe a little too quick.

"But, I'm sort of seeing Craig Hampton."

"Craig Hampton!" I couldn't hold in my disbelief. He was the captain of the football, hockey, and baseball teams. My friends and I called him "The Mayor" behind his back because he walked around the school like he ran it. The guy was a complete jerk with no personality. Why any girl would like him was beyond me.

"How can you go out with that guy? He's such a jerk." I wanted to say worse, I was so angry.

"Craig's not a bad guy. You don't know him like I know him. He's actually really nice." I couldn't believe she was saying the old "You don't know him like I do." I hate that line!

"I know I don't know him like you do. I know the locker room Craig, not the one who put you under some spell."

Maria exploded at this statement and shot back, "You should talk, Orville Jacques. You become a big star and you tell everyone that it's not going to your head and what do you do? You take Kim Archer to the governor's dinner. Don't talk to me about spells! Enjoy class, you're late."

Maria stormed down the hallway.

I just stood there. I couldn't believe it. It was something out of one of those teenage movies, but it was real, and it had happened to me. I knew Maria was right. Who was I to criticize her? My actions caused this. At the end of the summer, I knew I had a chance with her, but I began playing mind games by ignoring her, and then I topped it off by bringing Kim Archer to the dinner. I thought, Why did I listen to Scotty and his advice? Who made him the expert—who did he ever date? I was desperately trying to shift the blame, but I knew there was only one person to blame: me.

I was about five minutes late for criminology class,

and the guest lecturer had already begun. Mrs. Carlson shot me a look just to inform me how rude I was showing up late for class. I just shrugged. I had no defense. She was right. I went over and sat in my chair, between Gina and Scotty.

"How'd it go?" Scotty and Gina whispered in both my ears.

"It didn't. I'll tell you later." I stared straight ahead at the retired police officer in the front of the room. I zoned out while the man talked about where he got his training and began defining different laws for Mrs. Carlson's benefit. I really wasn't paying any attention to the poor guy until he began taking questions and Gina raised her hand.

"Yes, young lady," he said with a smile.

"Yes, Officer Walker. As you know, sitting next to me is Orville Jacques." I popped my head up at the sound of my name.

"Well, we all know Orville solved those murders this past summer. I was wondering, are there any other unsolved murders for good old Orville to solve?" Everyone laughed except me. I was a little embarrassed.

"Well, yes. There are many cases on the Cape that have stumped detectives. Robberies, missing persons, arson, murder. The list goes on and on. But, I don't want to discourage you, Mr. Jacques. We can always use a few good men." Mrs. Carlson gave him a look, and he added with a smile, "And we can always use a few good women." The class laughed. I gave him a smile and a nod.

"Can you tell us about other cases?" Scotty Donovan asked.

"I suppose we have time to talk about one. You see, in the last class I kind of got off track and that's all I talked about. But, I guess we have time for one case. What topic do you want to know about, son?" he asked Scotty.

"Murder."

"I thought you were going to say that. I'll tell you about one that not many know about or even talk about." Mr. Walker had the attention of the whole class, even people who had spent the entire class passing notes to each other.

"The year was 1946. It was before my time in police work, but I remember it clearly though because back then no one was ever murdered, and it sent shock waves throughout the Cape."

"What happened?" Scotty was always in a rush.

"Ssh." The class echoed.

"It was a beautiful July night, and there was a dance in the hall by the harbor. They tore the dance hall down back in the sixties. Well, anyway there was a young woman named Katherine Stinson who was with a group of her roommates. They were all sharing a house for the summer. Near the end of the dance, Katherine told one of her friends that she was going to go for an ice cream soda with a man whom she had just met named Lawrence. She said Lawrence was outside waiting for her. Katherine didn't come home that night or the next day. She was reported missing by her roommates, and a search began for Katherine and Lawrence, the mystery man. Three days later a man found Katherine's body in the cranberry bogs up the street from Cranberry Beach. She had been strangled. Her clothes were torn but nothing was missing except her engagement ring." The class was mesmerized, but something was gnawing at me.

"Mr. Walker." I raised my hand.

"Yes, Mr. Jacques." Mr. Walker waited for my question but the bell interrupted me. It was one of the few times I have ever been in class and heard a chorus of groans when the bell has gone off.

The class applauded Mr. Walker and then headed for the door. I told Gina and Scotty that I'd meet them outside in ten minutes. I had to talk to Mr. Walker, and I wanted to be alone. Mrs. Carlson thanked Mr. Walker, and then he headed out the door.

"Mr. Walker." I stopped him in the hallway.

"Yes, Mr. Jacques." He turned almost like he was expecting me.

"Why did Katherine Stinson go with Lawrence if she was engaged?" I asked, for some reason out of breath.

"That was the question everyone in town asked. Why would she go anywhere with a man if she was engaged? No one found that answer, Mr. Jacques." He walked toward the door to the parking lot.

"Wait. Mr. Walker what was the name of her fiancé? I mean he must've been a suspect."

"For the life of me, I can't remember. I do remember many believed he'd done it. To tell you the truth, I don't remember much about the case. I began telling the class because I knew we'd run out of time before we got to the technical stuff. I just wanted to get everyone on the edge of their seats. I think it worked." He winked and opened the door. It worked all right! As he was shutting the door behind him he stopped.

"Will. Will Michaels. That's it." He snapped his fingers.

"What? What did you say?" I had to hear it again.

"Katherine Stinson's fiancé's name was Will Michaels. I remember now because he was a detective and pretty well respected, but then Katherine was found dead and it ruined his career. Well anyway, I've got a three o'clock tee time. Good to talk to you, Mr. Jacques." He shut the door.

"Yeah, thanks, Mr. Walker," I said, stunned. I slowly took the watch that Will had given me for a gift off my wrist. It had been his watch. It had meant a lot to him. It was given to him by a woman—a woman I never dared ask about because I didn't want him to get depressed. Now I didn't have to ask him. I read the inscription like I did every day.

"To Will, Love, Katherine."

This time it meant more than lost love; it meant murder . . .

CHAPTER THREE

THE BELLTOWN Library had joined the twentieth century since my last visit. The copies of the *Belltown News* used to be stacked in the cellar, but now they were on microfilm. This would make my job a lot easier. I scanned through the file cabinet until I found a case that read *Belltown News* June 1 to December 31, 1946. I grabbed the case and went over to one of the new microfilm machines. I sat down and fumbled with the machine for ten minutes, but it was as foreign to me as my Spanish homework. The librarian, who had been watching me struggle, couldn't take it anymore. She got up from her desk and came to rescue me.

"Having trouble, young man?"

"Yes, ma'm. I'm not the most mechanical guy."

"That's OK. This is very easy, once you get the hang of it." She smiled and gave a reassuring nod.

"Now, what are you looking for?"

"July of 1946."

"That was long before me. What's the topic?" she asked.

"Actually, I guess you could say the topic is murder. A woman's body was found in a cranberry bog back in 1946."

"Wow. How horrible. Why are you looking it up?"

I was prepared for this question. "Well, we talked about it in criminology class today because it remains unsolved. So my teacher said if anyone wanted extra credit to write a brief paper." I could tell the topic fascinated the librarian. Her mind was working.

"You know, there's an elderly woman who helps out in the children's section. She's lived in Belltown most of her life. I bet she could help you," the librarian offered.

"Oh, thanks, but that's OK. I wouldn't want to bother her."

The truth is, I didn't want to include any more people. I wanted to find my information and be on my way.

"Really, you wouldn't be bothering her. She loves to help the students, and this would be right up her alley. She was probably in her early twenties back then. I'll go get her."

The librarian took off before I could answer. Normally, I would have been grateful. She was certainly going above and beyond her call of duty. But, I really wanted to do my own thing. I saw the librarian walk over to the children's section of the library and say something to a woman who was stacking books. She pointed at me, and the woman nodded, put down some books, and came my way.

"Hi, young man. Mrs. Herman said I might be able to help you with some Belltown history," the woman said.

"Well, yeah, maybe. It was July of 1946."

"Hmm...July of 1946. I was twenty-fi ... one. Well, let's just say I was in my twenties," she said with a laugh.

"Let's first get this microfilm into the machine." She put the film in the machine in twenty seconds. A feat I hadn't even come close to accomplishing.

"OK. Now when you push this button, it turns the pages. And if you want to copy anything, you push this button and pay for your copies at the front desk. Now what are you looking for from July of 1946? Your grandparents' wedding? Or maybe when one of your parents were born? What's you grandparents' surname?"

"Oh, no. Nothing like that. The librarian didn't tell you?"

"No, I just figured it was something like that. That's what I usually help the kids with because I know a lot of their parents and grandparents. So what are you looking up?"

"Actually, I'm looking up the unsolved murder of Katherine Stinson. Her body was found in a cranberry bog back in 1946." The woman turned her head for a moment.

She didn't say anything.

"Did you know her, Ms. . . ." She turned and faced me again.

"Mrs. Mahoney . . . No . . . I . . . didn't know her, Mr. . . . uh . . ."

"Jacques. Orville Jacques." I wasn't trying to but I sounded just like James Bond.

"Oh, you're the boy from the summer murders."

"Yes. Do you remember the Katherine Stinson case?" I got right to the question; my cover had been blown.

"No, I don't remember anything. 1946 was so long ago." I read Mrs. Mahoney's face and her body language. She was very uneasy, and it looked like she had seen a ghost.

"Yeah, I know 1946 was so long ago, but I doubt there were many murders back then." I didn't let up. She had to remember the case. Why didn't she want to talk about it?

"I vaguely recall a woman found dead, but that's it. Why are you digging this up anyway?"

"Oh, just a class project. Thanks for all your help, Mrs. Mahoney."

Mrs. Mahoney nodded and made her escape. "Why are you digging this up?" I said to myself. She didn't say, Why are you looking this up? She said "digging." That word told me how she felt. She didn't like the idea that I was digging. And there was one other word that stood out, "vaguely." She vaguely remembered a murder. Come on!

I forgot about Mrs. Mahoney when I came to July

19,1946.The headline and article made Mr.Walker's story in crim class a reality:

>Belltown Summer Resident Feared Abducted
>
>Authorities began a search today by land, sea, and air. Miss Katherine Stinson, 24, of Boston, who vanished from Belltown Dance Hall July 17 with a man known only as Lawrence.
>
>Mystery Man Sought
>
>A posse under the command of State Trooper Roger F. Potter, Jr., and police Chief John L. Davenport of Belltown has begun searching the woods and ocean in the vicinity of the dance hall. State detectives are asking for any information about a man named Lawrence who was at the dance. During the intermission of the dance, Miss Stinson told her roommate, Mary Brandon: "I just met a man named Lawrence. We're going to Dale's Diner for some ice cream sodas. I shouldn't be home too late, so wait up if I'm not home by the time you're home."
>
>Engaged to Detective
>
>At the time of Miss Stinson's disappearance, she was wearing a diamond engagement ring given to her by State Detective Will Michaels of Boston. Detective Michaels is highly decorated from his service in World War II and has served as a state detective for two years. Detective Michaels was unavailable for comment. When last seen, Miss Stinson, a nurse at Boston City Hospital, was wearing a blue dress, a white sweater, and blue shoes.

I pushed the button and copied the page. I pushed page turner button a couple of times and read headlines like "Woman Still Missing" and "Search Continues for Missing Woman." I stopped when I came to July 22, 1946:

Woman's Body Found in Bog

A body believed to be that of Katherine Stinson was found in Coolidge Cranberry Bogs, which are a quarter of a mile from Cranberry Beach. Miss Katherine Stinson, a 24-year-old nurse from Boston, had been missing for three days. She was last seen at the Belltown Dance Hall before leaving with an unidentified man whom she referred to as Lawrence.

The body was discovered floating in the Cranberry Bogs Reservoir by Peter Matthews of Belltown, who notified Belltown police at 7:21 AM. Police Chief John L. Davenport was the first policeman at the scene, which is located approximately three miles from the Belltown Dance Hall.

The body was removed from the water at 9:22 AM under the direction of Belltown County Medical Examiner Michael P. Hughes. Dr. Robert W. Wilson, pathologist of the state department, was called from Boston to make an investigation.

Peter Matthews, of 62 Blueberry Lane, who works at the Coolidge Cranberry Bogs, said he passed the reservoir on his way to his job.

Police Identify Clothes

Although state police officials identified the clothing on the body as similar to that worn by

Miss Stinson, they said positive identification remains to be made. Since Miss Stinson was an orphan, the police are waiting on the identification by her fiancé, State Detective Will Michaels.

About the Victim

Miss Audrey Baxter, one of the victim's summer roommates, gave the Belltown News a brief history of Katherine Stinson yesterday. "Katherine was such a wonderful person. She's had a tough life. She was born in a small town in Kansas named Bewley. Her parents were farmers, and she was their only child. Her parents died when the farm burned down when she was only sixteen. She was all alone, an orphan. But, she went to nursing school, and then she moved north and became a great nurse. She was so loving and she just wanted to help people. She didn't have one enemy in the world."

I kept reading on. There was no indication of the exact cause of death, and everything else was about the search for the man whom Katherine Stinson referred to as Lawrence. There was one other thing that stuck out that I took note of. Her engagement ring was missing. The article mentioned that her pocketbook with her rent money was intact. Her clothes and shoes were also intact. But, her engagement ring was missing. The thought that went through my head tore my heart right out of me. I didn't want to think those thoughts. I put all my stuff in my backpack, paid for my copies, and headed for home.

As I plodded away at my algebra that night, the thoughts came back to me. I had a hypothesis, but I didn't want to believe it. I couldn't avoid it, though. I threw my homework to the side and wrote the sequence of events down in my detective notebook.

1. An unknown decorated policeman tells me, "Will Michaels was a dirty cop."

2. Mr. Walker said about the Katherine Stinson murder, "I do remember that many believed he [Will] had done it."

3. Why would Katherine Stinson leave the dance with a man if she was engaged to Will?

4. Why would someone take her engagement ring and leave her pocketbook, which had her rent money.

Robbery couldn't have been the motive. My pen shook as I put my hypothesis on paper.

Will probably had to work, so he didn't go to the dance with Katherine. Katherine was angry or something, so she left the dance with a guy named Lawrence. Maybe her feelings were changing about Will. Will got off work and was about to enter the dance when be saw Katherine and Lawrence leaving. This set Will off. He snapped. He followed them and then, when they parked, he killed them. He took the engagement ring off of Katherine as a symbol. She wasn't worthy of his love or something.

I read over my hypothesis and was shivering at how realistic it looked. A couple of questions popped into my head. Why would he put her in the cranberry bogs? What did he do with Lawrence? I answered them almost as quickly as I had asked them. The Coolidge Cranberry Bogs are a quarter of a mile up the street from Cranberry Beach. Lawrence and Katherine were probably in the car watching the moonlight, even kissing. Will killed them and threw Katherine into the bogs so she would not be found for a few days. He disposed of Lawrence somewhere else, so it would look like the unknown Lawrence was the killer. If anyone could pull something like that off, a state detective could. What scared me the most about my hypothesis was that I was so quick to believe it. I knew I had to make a conscious effort not to judge Will, yet! I also knew I couldn't let this lie. I had to find the truth. There were a couple of other things that were bothering me:

  1. What was Mrs. Mahoney's deal? I knew she knew something.

  2. Something Audrey Baxter had said about Katherine Stinson didn't seem to ring true to me.

  I tried to get in touch with Shane O'Connell for two days, but he was either busy in meetings or out of the office. Every good detective needs someone on the inside, and Shane was my connection at the Belltown Police Station. Shane had helped me in my first murder case, and everyone in Belltown had found out. He took a lot of heat because he let a sixteen-year-old kid stay on a murder case when he knew there could be danger. Shane didn't deserve that kind of treatment. He treated me like an equal. That's what I liked about him most. But after he didn't return any of my calls, I kind of got a little worried that he didn't want to be my man on the inside, so I decided to go to his office.

I knocked on the door and Shane said, "Yeah, come on in." I opened the door and Shane was sitting behind a mountain of paperwork. "So what's up? I know you've been trying to call me, but "I'm being killed with paperwork."

"I'm glad to hear that."

"Glad to hear it?"

"What I mean, Shane, is I thought you were avoiding me, 'cause everybody gave you a hard time about that case."

"Hey, who cares what they think. We solved the case. I'd do it the same way again if I had to."

"That's good because I need your help, again."

"You gotta be kidding. More murders in this town?"

"Well there was one."

"When?" he demanded.

"1946."

Shane laughed, "1946. What are you talking about?"

"Before you laugh me out of here, listen. There's an unsolved murder from 1946, and I think I'm onto something."

"OK, speak. I'll give you five minutes." Shane folded his arms. He was skeptical, but in ten minutes his attitude changed.

"And you think Will has something to do with Katherine Stinson's death?"

"I don't want to think that, but things are beginning to point that way." It hurt me to say it.

"Orville, I think I told you once that Will Michaels saved my father. He's not a killer."

"That's right. I was going to ask you about that. How'd he save your dad? Was it on duty?" I asked.

"Well, military duty. My dad wasn't a cop. He was a dentist."

"Really?" I was surprised. I always assumed Shane's dad was a cop.

"You see, Orville, my dad was only sixteen when he served in World War II. He lied about his age. Well, anyway, Will was in his platoon and kind of looked out for him since they both were from Boston. One night they were under heavy attack and one of the guys lost it and began to shoot at anything in his sight. He was aiming at my father's back, and Will jumped in front of my father and took three bullets meant for my dad's back. That's why Will has that severe limp."

"If he got that limp from being shot in the war, how did he become a detective?"

"His dream in life was to be able to work in law enforcement, so the town council gave him a special dispensation. They felt he deserved it for his courage, and that's my point. Will Michaels wanted to protect lives, not take them. He's not a killer, Orville."

"Believe me, I don't want to believe that, Shane. But, I have to find out more about this."

"All right, I understand your curiosity. So, what do you want me to do for you?"

Shane said the words I wanted to hear. I knew he understood my burning desire to know the truth.

"I was reading the old articles about the case, and I was wondering if you could put Katherine Stinson's name in the computer and get her date of birth and her parents' names and all that kind of stuff."

"This isn't 'Magnum PI.' I can't just put her name in the computer and it will spit out her favorite color and who her prom date was. I need to at least know where she was born."

"Shane, give me a little credit. She lived in Bewley, Kansas," I said, while handing him a piece of paper with the information.

" Oh, OK, that shouldn't take too long. I'll do it later on—I really gotta get back to this paperwork. But, Orville, what good is it to know her date of birth and parents' names?"

"I don't want to say why I want to know. I have a tiny theory, and I don't want to jinx it. Thanks a lot, Shane, I really appreciate this."

"Well, let's just keep it our little secret, OK?" Shane stressed secret.

"Naturally. Our little *secret*." I nodded in agreement.

CHAPTER FOUR

I STILL HADN'T heard from Shane, and I was getting a little anxious, but I knew I shouldn't pressure him. He had been busy, and if he said he'd get me the information, he would. I had to give him time. Time. That was something I didn't want to waste. Just because I was waiting on Shane didn't mean I had to stop investigating. I had wrestled with the thought for two days, and I finally decided I had to break into Will's apartment and see what was in that shoe box. I know Will's a friend and you don't invade a friend's privacy. But I knew whatever was in the shoe box had to do with his past. And it really wouldn't be breaking in because he gave me a key just to have in case of an emergency. I considered this an emergency. I knew I was justified.

Will left his apartment at 6:30 PM to go and play

bingo at St. Jude's. St. Jude's was about a fifteen-minute walk, but because of Will's limp, it would probably take him about twenty-five minutes to get there. Bingo was from 7:00 to 9:00. That meant I had more than enough time to find the shoe box. When Will was finally out of sight, I unlocked the door and felt for the light switch. I turned on the lights and scanned the TV room—no shoe box. I went into his bedroom and there it was, right on the nightstand by the bed. I was surprised I found it so quickly, and it kind of took me off guard. I hesitated a little before I opened the box. My conscience was making me rethink what I was doing, but I had come this far, so I opened the box. In the shoe box was a stack of letters with an elastic band around them. There must've been thirty letters, and each one began "Dear Will" and ended "Love always, Katherine."The letter on the top of the stack was dated July 14, 1946. That was just a little more than a week before Katherine's body was found. I read:

> Dear Will,
>
> I was just talking to Audrey about the wedding, and it struck me that five months ago today you made me the happiest woman in the world by asking me to marry you. I will never forget that night at the Valentine's dance in Boston. They were playing our song, and you got on one knee and told me that you would love me forever. I am writing you this letter to tell you how much I love you. I know I tell you that all the time, but I want this on paper. You came into my life when I thought

I could never let anyone come close to me again. I fought your love, not because I didn't want it, because I did. I was afraid to love anyone in fear that I would lose him. So, I fought you, but you didn't resist. You taught me what true love is all about. You showed me that there is still goodness in this world. Will Michaels, I want you to know, I will mean it when I say the word "forever" at our wedding. I will mean forever as long as eternity and beyond that.

Love always,
Katherine

I folded up the letter and put it back in the stack and wrapped the elastic band around it. I had made a terrible mistake. I felt sick to my stomach. I had betrayed my friend by searching through his personal things. Also, reading her words, it was obvious how much in love she was with him. They were going to have a wonderful life together, a life filled with love. I had to put Will's shoe box back just as I had found it. I was shaking with guilt as I began to put it on his nightstand, thinking that all this great man had of this love was a stack of letters in a shoe box.

"Orville, what are you doing?"

Startled I dropped the box, and the letters fell on the floor.

"Will, I'm sorry I just . . ." What could I say?

Will limped over to the letters and began picking them up. "I figured you'd hear about it sometime. I just thought we were close enough that you could ask me," he said sadly as he put the letters into the box.

"I'm sorry." I looked down on the floor, avoiding eye contact. That's when I saw it. My eyes bulged out of my head. I reached down for it, but he grabbed it before I could.

"That ring! That's an engagement ring! Oh, my God, Will! That's Katherine's ring! Isn't it? Will! Why? Did you?" I yelled.

"Yes. That's Katherine's ring. I keep it with me all the time." He didn't raise his voice. It was as though he was in a trance and wasn't concerned about my yelling.

"That night she was murdered. Her ring. Her ring was missing. Why, why Will? Why Will? Did you? Did you? . . ."

Will came out of his trance and finished my question. "Did I kill Katherine?" He looked right into my eyes. "Is that what you want to know?" Will began a slow, frustrated laugh.

"Yes. That's want I want to know." I couldn't let up.

"After forty something years that question is still being asked. If you want to know the truth, come into the other room."

Will limped into the TV room and went over to an old phonograph and got a record off the shelf. He cued the record and it began to play. He closed his eyes for a couple of seconds and took the music in and began singing some of the words to a slow song.

I'll never smile again until I smile at you..
I'll never laugh again, What good would it do?

"Do you hear this song, Orville?" Will asked, eyes shut.

"Yes."

"I play this song whenever I want Katherine here. This was her favorite Frank Sinatra song. This was our song. We used to dance to it or sing it when we were driving down from Boston to the Cape. This was our song, Orville." Tears began to roll down his cheeks as he sang.

> *I'll never love again, I'm so in love with you.*
> *I'll never thrill again to somebody new.*
> *Within my heart*
> *I know I will never start*
> *To smile again until I smile at you.*

Will opened his eyes and they were filled with tears. The song was still playing, but it was the instrumental part meant for a slow dance.

"The night before . . ." His voice cracked a bit. "The night before it happened, we were driving in my car. I began singing our song. She always would join in. She didn't. She began to cry. She took the ring off her finger and gave it to me. She said she couldn't marry me." There was a steady stream of tears rolling down his cheeks.

"Why?" I asked as the song ended and brought Will out of his trance.

"Why?" He stared at me. "Why? . . . Why? I've been asking why for years. Sometimes I wake up at night in a cold sweat yelling, 'Why?' She said she loved me, Orville. She said she'd love me forever. That night, she gave me back the ring, she said she was mistaken. Mistaken, Orville. That word will also stay with me forever." He took out a handkerchief and wiped his eyes.

"When the newspaper reported that her engagement ring was missing, why didn't you tell them that she had given it back to you?"

"It was none of their business. I go to sleep every night with the same questions. 'Did she ever love me?' and 'Why did she leave the dance with Andrew MacNichol?' Not knowing the truth is paralyzing." He dropped his head.

"I thought they said the guy's name was Lawrence?"

"He said his name was Lawrence that night. His name was Andrew MacNichol. He went to trial but wasn't convicted."

"Where is he now?"

"I have no idea where the …" He stopped himself, gritted his teeth, and continued "where he is now."

"Why do people think that … you killed her?"

"You can answer that. Why did you think that?" He gave me a cold stare.

"Well, I thought you probably saw her with another man, and you were jealous." I felt terrible giving my answer.

"That's what a lot of people thought. Even though I had witnesses saying I was in Boston. That really didn't matter to the gossips. They figured I had to be in on it somehow. And when they couldn't prove it, my own people framed me a year later saying I was taking bribes. They set me up to satisfy the community. I spent three years in prison, and everyone felt justice was somewhat served. Even if they couldn't get me for murder, they still got me behind bars."

His sadness turned into anger. "Orville, in all these years, you were the only real friend I have had. You were like the son I dreamed Katherine and I would have had, and now I catch you sneaking through my house looking for proof. You're just like the rest. In fact, you're worse. They never trusted me. I gained your trust, or so I thought, and this is how I'm repaid. I want you to leave me alone. I don't ever want you to come here again." He pointed at the door.

"Will, I'm sorr . . ."

"Don't say that word. Just leave me in peace."

There was nothing I could say, so I walked toward the door. I began to turn around, but his voice stopped me.

"Don't turn around. Leave, now."

I paused for a second. The room was silent except for the sound of the needle indicating that the record was over.

I shut the door and I couldn't hold it in. I felt myself crying—something I hadn't done since my grandfather died. I hadn't trusted a friend. A friend who had taught me so much. I had been just like the rest of them. Orville Jacques, the great detective, I thought. It was one time in my life that I really hated being Orville Jacques . . .

CHAPTER
FIVE

WHEN I GOT home from school the next day, I just wanted to take a nap because I really felt lousy about a million things: 1. Will 2. Maria 3. Mr. Reasons' comment on my algebra test: "Not even worth grading." I grabbed my Walkman and was going to head upstairs when I found a message from my mom on the kitchen table. It read: "Shane O'Connell called. Come by the station A.S.A.P." I was halfway out the door before I finished reading it. "Also, bring in the barrels." I grabbed the four trash barrels and put them in the backyard. I unlocked my mountain bike and headed for the Belltown Police Station.

When I got there, Shane was sitting behind his desk, and there were only a couple of folders left on it.

"I see you put a dent in the paperwork." I smiled.

Shane nodded, smiled, and got down to business.

"Take a seat, Orville. It was because of all this paper-work that it took me so long to check on the information you wanted about Katherine Stinson. Also, I really didn't see what good it would be to check on where this woman was born and her parents and all that stuff." He opened his drawer and pulled out a manila folder.

"And?" I said, sitting on the edge of my seat.

"And check this out. There was only one Katherine Stinson born in Bewley, Kansas." He slid a folder across the desk. I looked at a copy of a birth certificate and a copy of a death certificate. It didn't make any sense.

"I don't get it, Shane. It says on the birth certificate that Katherine Stinson was born January 5, 1921. And on the death certificate it says she died January 10, 1921. That's five days after she was born." I was puzzled.

"Exactly. Probably crib death. Pretty sad, huh?"

"Well, yeah, of course. But, I still don't get it. This couldn't be our Katherine Stinson." I was lost.

"Exactly. That's the point. There's no way this was our Katherine Stinson, but she said she came from Bewley, Kansas. That means . . ."

"She lied." I jumped in.

"You got it. Her real name wasn't Katherine Stinson. She took Katherine Stinson's name and gave herself an identity, which was probably not that hard to do back then."

"But why?" I asked.

"That's the million dollar question, Orville. Why did she change her name and background? What was she hiding from? Maybe her real name has something to do with . . ."

"Her death." I jumped in again.

"That's right. I can't believe you got me going again." Shane sighed.

"What I don't understand is why no one checked on this back in 1946." I shook my head.

"Well, first of all, she told everyone she was an only child and her parents were dead. So, there really was no one to notify. Also, the world was a lot different back then. If a woman told you she was an orphan from Kansas you would have believed her. Now there are all the crazy stories about the quiet neighbor next door who turns out to be wanted in ten states." Shane leaned back in his chair.

"Now what?"

"I'm going to get the old files of the case, and I'm going to ask a few questions of the old locals. And you, my friend, are going to stay out of this one. This might not pan out. Who knows, maybe Katherine Stinson was who she said she was, and the Bewley Town Hall just misplaced her birth certificate. But, if I start finding stuff out, I don't want to be responsible for your safety."

"Whatever," I said offended.

"Orville, don't whatever me. I'm serious. Promise me you won't poke around."

"All right," I lied.

"Good."

"But, you have to update me if you find anything."

"OK." He nodded. I think he lied, too, but what could I say?

"I'll see you later." I got up to leave.

"Wait. I want to know, how did you think to have me check her birth certificate?" He was intrigued.

"In that article I read, Katherine's friend Audrey said that Katherine grew up on a farm, and she was an only child. Well, I know from my U.S. history class that farmers back then had large families, so they could help maintain the land. Not all, but most. So, that intrigued me. I thought maybe Katherine had a couple of brothers or sisters that she didn't want anyone to know about, and maybe they knew something about her death. I guess I was wrong."

"Only child on a farm. Orville, that was a great instinct. Some day, you'll be a good detective."

"Yeah, some day," I muttered to myself.

After I left the police station, I rode my bike to Cranberry Beach. I guess I just wanted to find a quiet place to think about everything that had happened. I sat on the jetty and watched the tired green waves ride up to the shoreline, How many times had those waves made that journey? I thought. And how many times had Will and Katherine watched that same ocean, walking hand-in-hand, planning their future. What had changed Katherine's mind? I knew it had nothing to do with her no longer being in love with Will. Her letter told me that she loved Will. People change and feelings change, but the letter was so real—they were in love. They would always be in love. Maybe, that was one of the reasons why Will ended up in a mental hospital. He couldn't find the truth, and it broke him.

Why did Katherine break off the engagement? Why did she leave the dance the next night with someone she didn't know? And the biggest question that ran through my mind was: If her real name wasn't Katherine, why did she change her name? I wondered if Will knew that she had changed it. If he didn't, I couldn't tell him. It was bad enough I betrayed his friendship. There was no way I was going to tell him the woman he loved wasn't who she said she was. As a light Fall rain began to fill the sea, I promised myself I had to find the truth, and some day, Will would never have to ask, "Why?"

Mr. Haggerty brought me out of my trance. "Hey, Orville. What'ya doing on the jetties?" he asked while pushing his metal detector along the beach.

"Oh, hi Mr. Haggerty. I just came here to think a little."

I jumped off the rocks and walked over. I felt sorry for Mr. Haggerty. His wife had passed away a couple of years before and his only child, Ray, had died in the Vietnam War.

"I come here, too, when I want to think. It's peaceful. Like being with God." He smiled.

"Yeah, you're right," I agreed as we both watched a seagull swoop down onto the jetty.

"So, Mr. Haggerty. I always see you with that metal detector. Do those things really work?"

"Oh, they sure do, Orville. I've been combing this beach for twelve years. Orville, I'm telling you, you wouldn't believe the things I've recovered. Jewelry, knives, license plates, you name it, I've found it."

"Really. That's pretty interesting."

"You think so?" He seemed surprised that I was interested, but I really was intrigued.

"Do you want to come over to my house and see my collection? I keep everything I find and put the date of when I found it. It's my little hobby. Would you like to see it?" He was a little excited.

"I really would but I can't today. I really have to go home."

"I understand," he said, dejected.

"I really would like to see your collection some other time." I said with enthusiasm. I knew he was lonely and just wanted some company, but I did have to go home.

"OK, Orville. I'm here at this beach every day, if you're in the neighborhood." He smiled.

"Sounds great, Mr. Haggerty. Take care." I smiled and headed for my bike. The rain, now harder, pattered the sea as Mr. Haggerty pushed the detector along the wet sand.

I couldn't believe how psyched I was to get to the Belltown Library the next day. Was this the same Orville Jacques who didn't do a history paper once because there was a Sherlock Holmes marathon on PBS? But, this visit to the library was not for school but for the real thing—murder. I knew I had to look up more articles from 1946 and find out who Andrew MacNichol was. When I found that out, I could then take the next step and find out where he was now.

I opened the file cabinet and looked for the microfilm case for the *Belltown News* from June 1 to December 31, 1946. 1 couldn't find it. In fact, the case from January 1 to June 1, 1947 was also missing. Since no one was at any of the machines, I figured someone must've used the film and forgot to put it back into the file cabinet. I walked over and checked all four machines—no film.

I was now getting suspicious and decided to check the other file cabinets with the microfilm for the *Boston Globe* and the *Cape Cod Times.* Two cases were missing in each cabinet. Two from June 1 to December 31, 1946, and two from January 1 to June 1, 1947. I felt a chill go up my spine, but I wasn't going to jump to conclusions. I went over to the front desk, where the young librarian was sitting, jotting something on a piece of paper.

"Excuse me," I said.

"Yes." She looked up.

"Hi. I don't know if you remember me, but the other day you got Mrs. Mahoney to help me look something up."

"Oh, yes. I remember you. It was about a murder from way back," she said while putting her pen down.

"To be exact, 1946. The thing is I wanted to look it up again, but the microfilm for that year seems to be missing."

"Really," she said, concerned, and got up out of her chair. We both walked over to the file cabinets and she searched them thoroughly. She turned to me and said, "After you used them the other day, you did put them back?"

"I'm positive. Also, I didn't even use the ones from the *Boston Globe* and the *Cape Cod Times* and cases from 1946 and 1947 are missing from their cabinets."

"That's really strange." She shook her head.

We went back to her desk and she checked some papers. "Sometimes if the microfilm gets damaged, we send it back to the company that services our machines. But, there is no paperwork to suggest that is the case here. I'm going to have to took into this. Until then, I'm really sorry, I can't help you." She frowned.

"Well, maybe Mrs. Mahoney can help. Is she around?"

"I really don't know." She turned to a woman who was checking out a book. "Has Audrey been in today?"

"No, I haven't seen her in a couple of days," the other woman answered.

"Audrey?" I said stunned.

"Yes. Audrey Mahoney."

Could it be? I thought. Could Audrey Mahoney be Audrey Baxter, Katherine Stinson's roommate?

"Could you tell me where Mrs. Mahoney lives?"

"Actually, that is against our policy."

I knew she was a little wary about giving me Mrs. Mahoney's address, since she didn't know me.

"I understand, but I really have to get this paper done."

"Well, I don't know. Maybe I could write a letter to

your teacher or something," she offered.

I was determined to get that address. As I was about to beg some more, I saw Mr. Powers watching us. He was head of custodians for the public schools and the library. He had also been my Little League coach. I motioned for him to come over and he did.

"Hi, Orville. How are you?"

Pretty good, Mr. Powers, I answered as I watched the librarian taking it all in.

"Bob, you know this boy?" she asked Mr. Powers.

"Sure do. Everyone knows Orville. He solved the big murder case this summer. But, I knew him long before that. He played second base for me back in Little League. But, I hear you played outfield for the junior varsity team last year." He turned to me.

"Yeah, I went to left field because I was sick of taking the short hops in the face," I said with a laugh, while watching the librarian who was writing on a scrap piece of paper.

"I think this is what you're looking for." She handed me the piece of paper and added, "You understand, you really have to be safe these days with all the crazy people."

"Of course, I do." I smiled at her and then turned my attention back to Mr. Powers.

"Well, I better get going," I said to him.

"You must be working on a big paper 'cause I saw you here the other day."

"You could say I'm working on something really big. I'll see you later, Mr. Powers." I smiled.

"See you later, Orville," Mr. Powers said as he leaned onto the librarians' counter.

I looked down at the piece of paper. It read: Audrey Mahoney, 36 Fisherman's Lane.

Fisherman's Lane was on my way home. I hopped on my mountain bike and rode into the salt air chill, but I wasn't cold because my detective juices were flowing.

It took about about ten minutes to bike to Fisherman's Lane, which overlooked Belltown Harbor. I spotted number 36 in no time. The house was a one-story Cape with a garden that had been put to rest for winter. As I locked my bike to the fence, I thought of what approach I should use with Mrs. Mahoney. Do I do the ol' Columbo approach and act like I don't know what's going on, or do I just get to the point? It didn't take me too long to decide, because of the way Mrs. Mahoney answered the door.

"I thought you would be coming." She sighed and motioned me to come in. I followed her into the house.

"I was just making a pot of tea. Would you like some?" Mrs. Mahoney went into the kitchen, and I looked at the pictures on the wall.

"Sure. I'd love a cup." I'm not much of a tea drinker, but I knew having a cup I could take my time drinking it and that would prolong my stay.

"So how did you know I was coming?" I raised my voice so she could hear me in the kitchen.

"I can't lie too well, and I knew you saw right through me." Mrs. Mahoney said from the kitchen. She then appeared with a tray. On it was a tea pot, two cups, and a basket of cookies.

"Anyway," she continued, "you're Belltown's boy detective." She put the tray on the coffee table and poured us both a cup. I grabbed a cookie and took a bite.

"Awesome cookie." I smiled.

"Thank you. But, let's get to the point. What do you want from me?" She put her cup down.

"You are Audrey Baxter? Aren't you?"

She frowned. "A long long time ago, before I met Jonathan Mahoney." My suspicions were confirmed.

"So Katherine Stinson was your roommate?"

"Kay, I used to call her Kay. Kay wasn't just my roommate—she was also my best friend."

"So she told you everything."

"Like a sister." Mrs. Mahoney smiled and took a sip of tea.

"Did she tell you . . ." I stopped for second. I wasn't sure if I should ask the question but then my instincts took over. "Did she happen to tell you her real name wasn't Katherine Stinson?"

Mrs. Mahoney gasped. "How did you know that?"

"Let's just say I figured it out. Did Will know her secret?"

"No. Will didn't know and that is what really bothered Katherine. When she met him she thought it was nothing serious, but then she fell in love with him. She couldn't tell him who she was."

"And who was she?" I fired the question.

"I don't know." I gave her an "I don't believe you" look.

"Really. I don't know. I found out that Katherine wasn't Katherine when I tried to get a list of her friends from Bewley to invite to the wedding. Katherine said to let it be, but I wouldn't let up. Finally, she swore me to secrecy and told me that her real name wasn't Katherine Stinson. I asked her what it was, and she said if she told me it would put me in danger. She said she was running from her past, and no one could ever find out who she was really was. Not even Will."

Mrs. Mahoney picked up her cup and took a long sip. I couldn't believe my hunch was right.

"So, why didn't you tell anyone about any of this when Katherine was found murdered? You didn't even tell Will. He's gone through his life thinking that she never really loved him." I was angry. Mrs. Mahoney began to cry, and I knew that she had struggled with her choice of secrecy. I felt guilty for yelling at her and judging her. I went over and awkwardly put my hand on her shoulder.

"I'm sorry. I'm really sorry, Mrs. Mahoney. I didn't mean to yell at you."

After a few seconds she said, "It's all right. You're right. I should've told someone, but I kept silent. I was afraid for my life. And I thought years later to tell Will, but I thought, what good would it do? I know I was wrong, but I didn't want anyone else to get hurt."

"Is that why you took the microfilm from the library, so I wouldn't stumble onto this? After all these years, do you think someone else could get hurt?"

"What do you mean, took the microfilm?" She looked puzzled.

"From the library. You know the microfilm I was looking at the other day."

"I was concerned that you were looking at the case, but I didn't take any of the microfilm from those years," she said.

"Well, someone did. They're missing."

"Someone must know you're looking into the case!" she exclaimed.

Someone who doesn't want me to, I thought.

"Orville, please stop checking on this. I still believe the killer is out there somewhere." She looked worried.

"Mrs. Mahoney, don't worry about me. I'll be just fine." I said to reassure her, but I didn't quite believe it myself.

"Now who was Andrew MacNichol?" I tried to continue acting like nothing was wrong, but that's not how I felt. I was getting a little scared.

"Andrew MacNichol's family owned a restaurant called the Fishing Hole. There was talk that it was a front and that his father had connections with the mob. That is why Andrew got off. But, I really don't want to talk about this anymore. Orville, believe me, you could be in danger." Mrs. Mahoney got up and opened the door for me.

"Why do you keep saying that? Maybe, the microfilm just got lost. This murder happened over fifty years ago."

"I'll tell you one more thing, Orville. And then I don't want you to come here again." She stared right into my eyes.

"OK. Fine." I nodded my head.

"You're not the only one who's tried to solve this murder."

"What do you mean?" I asked.

" Do you remember back in the late eighties Jack Pervis, a reporter for the *Cape Cod Times?*" She almost whispered.

"The name sounds familiar."

"He was reported missing."

"Oh, yeah, I was pretty young but I remember. He was reported missing but he had taken all the money out of his bank account, and everybody thought he just took off. Some people said he was into drugs and was a runner for a drug cartel."

"Yes. That was the most ridiculous story in the world. I knew Jack Pervis. He was a young up-and-coming investigative journalist. He told me that the story he was working on would get him out of Beiltown, and he would be writing for *Time* magazine. That was the day he asked me about Katherine. He said he was getting close to the truth, and it would be in the paper in about a week. The next day he was reported missing. Orville, please let it go. You could be in serious danger. Let the past be the past."

"OK, Mrs. Mahoney. I'll let it go." I nodded and walked out the door. I didn't know what my next step was, but I did know one thing: There was no way I was going to let it go, it had been let go long enough ...

CHAPTER
SIX

It was impossible to sleep that night. My mind whirling with the new information. Mrs. Mahoney confirmed a lot, but also gave me a new piece to the puzzle: Jack Pervis. Did Jack Pervis uncover Katherine Stinson's killer? Another thing that waved a red flag before my eyes was Andrew MacNichol's family's connection with the mob. If he was connected with the mob, no wonder he got off, I thought. I knew it would be a long day when I turned off my alarm five minutes before it was supposed to go off.

Mr. Reasons, my algebra teacher, cured my insomnia when he began his monotone lecture on algebra. My head bobbed as I tried desperately to keep my eyes open. But, focusing on all the crazy numbers and formulas and hearing his "You're getting very sleepy" voice was a losing battle and my eyelids finally caved in. I don't know how long I was out, a minute or ten. It didn't matter because once you fall asleep in class, everybody knows. I awoke to Mr. Reasons hovering above me, yelling, "Wake up, Mr. Jacques!" I jumped, and then hurried to fix my glasses, which had slid off my nose. Everybody was laughing, even Maria, who was sitting across the room. In the past, I might have been really embarrassed, but today I just rolled with it. Mr. Reasons looked excited. It wasn't often he made the class laugh with him.

"Well, Mr. Jacques. I hope I'm not boring you."

"Actually," I paused, "Mr. Reasons, this was probably one of your more interesting classes." The classroom echoed with laughter but was quickly silenced by Mr. Reasons raising his hand for order. I knew I probably shouldn't have said it, considering the man couldn't laugh at himself. I was right.

"Mr. Jacques . . ." I knew the look in his eyes said "after school," but before he could continue the intercom interrupted him. It was the principal, Mr. Finn.

"Good afternoon. I just have a few quick announcements. I normally wait until the end of the day, but I know you're dying to hear the results of Homecoming Queen and King. But first, the other announcements." We shifted in our seats through the regular announcements. Then Mr. Finn continued, "Now, the results. The votes have been counted, and this is a historical moment for Belltown High."

Mr. Finn sometimes got a little carried away.

"For the first time since we've opened the Homecoming Contest to the lower grades five years ago, we actually have two winners who aren't seniors. I would like to congratulate Orville Jacques and Maria Simpkins for winning the honor of being this year's Homecoming King and Queen. Thank you and have a good day."

I was now wide awake. But, it felt as though I was dreaming. All the girls in class were hugging Maria and patting her on the back. I got high fives from the guys. Mr. Reasons looked defeated. He knew it wouldn't be a popular choice to have me stay after school, so he tried to work a little sarcasm.

"Do you think, Mr. Jacques, you can stay awake during Friday afternoon's parade?"

I looked at Maria. She was all smiles as our eyes met.

"I don't think that will be a problem . . ." I kept my eyes on Maria. "I don't think that will be a problem at all." I gave her a quick smile and then turned my attention back to Mr. Reasons, who was already writing the next problem on the chalkboard.

I thought about Homecoming the rest of the school day, but when the bell rang, I knew I had to put it out of my head. There was a more pressing matter, even more pressing than Maria: the case. I thought I should go see Shane and try to find out if he had any leads. When I got to the police station, Shane was nowhere to be found. I figured he was probably getting a cup of coffee or something, so I went into his office and took a seat. After about five minutes, I was getting a little antsy, so I decided to write him a note to call me. I went over to his desk to find some paper and that's when I saw it. It was a brown folder labeled, "KATHERINE STINSON, MURDER CASE #0231. Property of Shane O'Connell." Wow, Shane had been gathering information on the case.

I had to think quick. Would Shane tell me what was in the folder? If he keeps me out in the cold I might never find out the truth, I thought.

The folder lay on the desk just waiting for me to take. I unzipped my backpack and began to justify my actions, something detectives are good at. "Hey, he shouldn't be so careless to leave the folder here lying on his desk." I think I said the same thing when my mom baked a chocolate cake once and left it on the kitchen counter. I stuffed the folder into the backpack and headed out of his office. Officer Jameson saw me walk out. He was standing at the water cooler, with a cup in his hands.

"Orville, are you looking for Detective O'Connell?"

"Yeah, I can't find him anywhere."

Officer Jameson looked down at his watch. "He's in a meeting with the chief and won't be done for a half hour."

"Oh, OK, I'll be back then. Thanks." I smiled.

"No problem." Officer Jameson continued down the hall. I couldn't believe my good fortune. I had a half hour to copy the documents in the folder and bring them back before he even caught on they were missing. I had to work quickly though. The folder must've had at least sixty pages. The Belltown Library was a ten-minute bike ride. There was no way I would be able to ride the bike there, copy the documents, and then ride back in less than a half hour. "Wait," I said to myself. "Dale's Video has a copy machine, and it's right across the street." I didn't even have to unlock my bike. I went across the street, copied each page, and paid Dale. The whole process took only fifteen minutes. It was a good thing, too, because as I was putting the folder on Shane's desk, his door opened.

"Nice try, Orville."

"What?" I faked innocence.

"Trying to sneak a look at the Stinson murder file." He took the folder from me.

"Well, you gotta give me credit for trying." I smiled.

"Oh, I give you credit. I'm just glad my meeting ended early. Ten minutes later and you would've had some theory on the murder." He put the folder in his desk and locked it.

"Does that mean you won't tell me what's in the folder?"

"Do you even have to ask that question?" He sat down in his chair and leaned back.

"I thought you were going to keep me updated?" I had to fake that I was disappointed or he might get suspicious.

"And I will. As of now, there is nothing new. When you look at a cold case like this one, the process can be lengthy. People who may have been key to the case may have died or moved. That's why I'm going to call an old friend at the FBI and see if he can track some names down for me. Until then, stop poking around my office and anywhere else you may have been."

"OK." I nodded.

Shane got out of his chair and showed me the door.

"If you were really only ten minutes later," I grumbled.

"But, I wasn't," Shane said proudly.

I knew having copies of the Katherine Stinson murder file could only help me. I jumped on my mountain bike, put on my Walkman and turned on a mix tape. I hummed along to The Samples melodic "Great Blue Ocean" as I biked past Cranberry Beach. I briefly visualized Will and Katherine in another time, a happier time. Then I forced myself to shake the thought out and focus on the case. I knew Shane was going to keep me out in the cold, but I felt I was definitely getting warm.

Thursday nights I usually had to do the dishes, but since the next day was the big Homecoming Parade and Pep Rally, my mom thought I should go through my wardrobe and pick out an outfit for the parade. "After all, Orville, you are representing the young men of your school, and you want to look good sitting next to that lovely Simpkins girl."

"Maria," I said.

"Yes, Maria. She is a lovely young woman. Well, you want to look good for her."

"Yeah, you're right." She couldn't have been more right. My dad and I went upstairs and went through my closet. It took us two minutes to find an outfit. I was just going to wear the same thing I wore at the governor's dinner except instead of a blue tie, I would wear a maroon one. The Belltown Pirates's colors were maroon and white. Since I didn't know how to tie ties, my dad tied it around his neck, and then loosened it and gave it back to me.

"There you go. You'll be all ready for tomorrow."

"Thanks, Dad. Now I can get to my homework," I was trying to get my father to leave. I really had no intention of doing my homework. I was just dying to look at the documents from Katherine Stinson's case.

"Are you OK, Orville?" My dad looked concerned.

"Yeah, why do you say that?"

"I've never seen you so excited to get to your homework."

"Well, maybe I'm maturing." I knew he would laugh at that.

"Yeah, right!" Dad laughed and shut the door behind him. Two seconds later, he opened the door again. "Orville, I knew I had something to tell you."

"What's that, Dad?"

"I bumped into Dr. Harris at the drugstore today."

"Yeah." I knew it was coming.

"She wanted to know if there was anything wrong between you and Will." My dad narrowed his eyes. He knew my expressions and came back into my room and shut the door.

"There is something wrong, Dad. Will got really mad

at me about something. Something that was between him and me."

"I won't ask you what it was about. But, did he have a reason to get mad at you?" Dad sat down on the edge of my bed while I settled into my chair.

"Yes. He had every reason to be angry."

Dad looked stunned, and he had to be wondering what I had done, but he asked, "Did you tell him you were sorry?"

"Yes, but it was right after the incident had occurred. Dad, I don't know what to do."

"Well, maybe he needed a little time to cool down. Maybe, you should try to apologize again."

"Yeah, but what if he doesn't want to listen to me . . ."

"Make him," Dad said firmly. "I have a feeling whatever it was you did or said, he probably wanted you to just think about it. I know he really values your friendship and wouldn't want to lose it. Make him chicken soup or something."

"Chicken soup?" I asked.

"Oh, yeah. I guess Will has had a bout with the flu. I know he could use your company." Dad opened the door.

"Dad."

"Yeah, Orville." He turned back.

"Thanks a lot." I smiled.

"No problem." He shut the door behind him. I felt a huge weight had been lifted off of me. I realized it was my place to face Will and tell him how sorry I was that I hadn't trusted him. I felt better about approaching Will. I would go to his apartment the next day after the parade and pep rally. I looked at the watch Will had given me. It was only 7:30, and I still had a few hours to read the murder files.

I read the files for about three hours, writing down things that I thought were important or intriguing me.

Andrew MacNichol didn't have a record of any kind. In fact, he was described as a "Good kid who does what he's told," by his father, Albert MacNichol, the owner of the Fishing Hole restaurant. The reason he was considered a suspect was that a 1945 Ford Beach Wagon was spotted on Cranberry Beach by Ben and Justine Beale at 10:15 the night of the disappearance. That was fifteen minutes before Katherine Stinson left the dance with the unidentified Lawrence. The car pulled out of Cranberry Beach and headed down Harbor Avenue, which was a oneway to Belltown Harbor. The car was the same make as the car Andrew MacNichol owned. Ben and Justine Beale described the driver. And when shown possible suspects in a line up, they picked number four, who was also Andrew MacNichol. Andrew MacNichol's car was searched, and strands of a woman's hair were found plus a small piece of blue fabric. The fingerpints all matched Katherine Stinson's. Also, the passenger door handle was missing. This meant the passenger could only get out if the door was opened from the outside.

So, if there was a struggle or any foul play in the car, there was no escape for the passenger. When police asked Andrew MacNichol how the handle broke off, he said, "Ask State Trooper Roger Potter." Under oath, State Trooper Roger F. Potter, Jr., said he was a longtime friend of the MacNichol family and was very embarrassed about how the handle broke. After being needled by the prosecutor, he admitted he had broken the handle off two nights before by mistake. He said, "I had been in an argument with my girlfriend and had a little too much to drink. Andrew drove me home from the Fishing Hole. I forgot the door was locked, and I kept pulling the handle real hard until it broke off." He added, smiling at Andrew, "I know I owe you a new handle." There was scattered laughter in the courtroom. Ben and Justine Beale later retracted their statements that Andrew MacNichol was the man they saw on that night. They also seemed confused on what kind of car they had seen. They said it could have been a Hudson and not a 1945 Ford Beach Wagon, the kind of car Andrew MacNichol owned. Lisa MacNichol testified that her son Andrew was home the entire night of the alleged incident.

Another thing I put in my notes: A copy of Katherine Stinson's will stated if she were to die, she wanted to be cremated and have her ashes cast off the jetties of Cranberry Beach.

I went over my notes and realized that Andrew MacNichol shouldn't even have been brought to trial. They had no concrete evidence on the guy. Yes, they found strands of a woman's hair in his car, a piece of material that matched Katherine Stinson's blue dress, and Katherine Stinson's fingerprints. That might mean she had been in the car, but that didn't mean murder. It was all circumstantial evidence. That didn't mean I thought the guy was innocent by any stretch of the imagination. There were a few things that really bothered me about the case:

1. Why would Ben and Justine Beale identify Andrew MacNichol and his car and then change their testimony?

2. I remembered that State Trooper Roger F. Potter, Jr., was in charge of the investigation to find the unidentified Lawrence. Wasn't it pretty coincidental that the man accused of murder was also his friend? Also, he testified that *he* broke the handle off the door and not Andrew MacNichol.

3. Katherine Stinson was only in her twenties and had her will drawn up. A will that stated if she were to die she wanted to be cremated and have her ashes cast off the jetties of Cranberry Beach. A woman so young was already thinking about death? It was like she saw the writing on the wall. Her murder must have had to do with her past.

I turned off my light and sat at my desk in the dark, sifting all the information in my mind. I had to find out if Ben and Justine Beale and Roger F. Potter, Jr., were still alive, and if they still lived in Belltown.

As I jumped into bed and pulled up the covers, I whispered the biggest question to myself.

"Where is Andrew MacNichol?"

It was a bitterly cold, gray day, and snow was forecast.

Still school officials didn't cancel the parade and pep rally though a moan echoed through the school after Mr. Finn announced everything was going ahead as planned. The only good part of having the parade meant it really was a nothing school day, since the band, football team, majorettes, and cheerleaders got out of classes to practice.

When the parade was ready to begin, Maria and I got in an old-fashioned, candy-apple-red Mustang convertible that Mr. Haggerty lent every year for the parade. Mr. Haggerty started up the engine.

"Are you ready, Orville and Maria?" he asked.

"Yup," we said together as we settled into the back seat.

"You two make a great couple." He smiled.

Embarrassed, I turned away. I knew my face was red, and it was not because of the cold weather.

"Thanks," Maria managed. I was trying to analyze her tone of voice, but I knew that would just drive me crazy, so I decided to forget about it.

Before we started off, Mr. Finn ran over to the car.

"Wait. Wait," he yelled. "You can't be Homecoming Queen without your crown." He handed me Maria's crown which looked like crystal but was really plastic.

"Orville, crown your queen," he ordered. He didn't know how right he was! I figured I wouldn't get a chance like it again, so I decided to play it up.

"I, King of the Belltown Pirates, hereby proclaim,

you, my fair maiden, Maria Simpkins, are the Queen of The Belltown Pirates." I put the crown on her head, and we both laughed at how stupid the whole thing was, but I have to admit, I loved every bit of it.

Mr. Haggerty drove about three miles an hour while Maria and I waved at the scattered crowd along the two-mile-long parade route. Snowflakes began to fall, and soon the snow was blowing along the street, dancing from side to side. I blew on my hands to warm my numb fingers. I couldn't believe I'd forgotten gloves.

When we approached Pirate Field where the pep rally was, the crowd was much larger. In the sea of familiar faces one stuck out. The glimpse was so quick that I wasn't sure it was him, but I thought I saw Will huddled behind a group of skateboarders. But, he's sick in bed with the flu, I thought. I looked back to double-check and I felt a hand touching my hand. It was Maria's.

"Orville, your hands must be freezing." She held my hand and rubbed it with her other hand.

"Yeah, a little. I, ah, forgot my gloves." I couldn't believe she was holding my hand. Maybe this was her way of forgiving me for our argument in the hallway. I didn't care why she was holding my hand. All I knew was she was holding *my* hand.

"Well, they're frozen. This will get the circulation going. But, I suggest that after the pep rally, you go with a bunch of us to Bill's Donuts and get some hot chocolate." Her smile warmed me up instantly.

"Yeah, that would be nice." I smiled back. The car pulled into Pirate's Field parking lot, and I opened her door and helped her out of the car.

"Thanks, Mr. Haggerty." I couldn't stop smiling.

"No problem. Hey, when are you coming by the house to see my metal detector collection?"

"In a few days. How's that?" I was so happy he could've asked me to paint his house, and I would have said yes.

"Are you ready to give your speech?" Maria asked as we walked to the field.

"Speech?" I said, stunned.

By the time I got home, I was beat. Maria and I had both given pretty good speeches, and we'd all had fun hanging out at Bill's Donuts afterward. But I felt a cold coming on, which was bad because the next day was the big game and the Homecoming Dance. There was no way I was going be sick and miss that. After all, the Homecoming King and Queen have the first dance. That meant I was guaranteed to dance with Maria at least once.

The next morning, my body ached. I was coughing and my nose was running a marathon. The disappointment was beginning to sink in until I opened my curtains and saw more snow. The radio told me what I had already guessed."The Belltown-Baywood game was postponed until tomorrow at 1:00 PM, weather permitting." I got back into bed and when I woke up around 2:30, I felt a little better. I didn't want to sleep anymore, so I got out my notes on the case and looked them over for a little while. Then I went downstairs and grabbed the

Cape Cod phone book. I looked up Benjamin and Justine Beale—no listing. Then I looked, Roger F. Potter, Jr.—no listing. And finally, I looked up Andrew MacNichol—no listing. I knew it was a long shot, but I was still kind of upset. Where do I go from here? I asked myself. I finally picked up the phone and dialed Gina's number.

"Hey, Gina what's up?"

"Nuthin' much, Orville. Just kind of bored sitting here watching the snow come down. Why? You wanna go sledding at the Country Club?"

"Nah. I'm sick."

"I really didn't want to go anyway. This snow is a waste. We hardly ever get any big snowstorms and sure enough, we get one on the weekend. What a waste, Orville. So, why did you call?"

"Well, I'm bored, too. But, I want to ask you for a favor?"

"Sure. What do you need?"

"Are you still into computers and all that stuff?"

"Let's just say, I could find out what the president had for breakfast. Does that answer your question?"

"Good, 'cause I need your help."

"Are you flunking algebra?" She laughed.

"Yeah, but what else is new." I laughed with her. "I have a few names for you. Do you have a pen?"

"Yeah. Hit me."

"Ben and Justine Beale." I paused, so she could write.

"Roger F. Potter, Jr., and Andrew MacNichol. Oh, and also, how about Jack Pervis." I spelled it for her.

"OK. Orville, so what do you want me to find out?"

"Their last known addresses or where they live now."

"No problem. But, Orville, you could probably be able to find that stuff out if you went to the Town Hall. This is no challenge to me." She laughed.

"I know, but I don't want to wait till Monday. I really appreciate this, Gina."

"I'll have what you need in ten minutes. But, Orville, what's this all about?"

"I was kind of hoping you wouldn't ask me that."

"All right, I'll let it go for now, but you know I'm going to get it out of you sooner or later."

"Later. Thanks, Gina." I hung up the phone. About ten minutes passed, and the phone rang again. I picked it up. "Eight minutes and twenty seconds. Not bad, huh?"

"Yeah."

"Gotta pen?"

"Yup." I opened my notebook.

"OK. First of all, Ben and Justine Beale lived on 1 Waterway Avenue from 1944 to 1988. Ben died in 1987."

"How'd he die?" I asked.

"Drowned. His boat capsized while he was fishing."

"Wow. What happened to Justine?"

"It says she's still alive. She lives in a nursing home in Brookline, Massachusetts. Do you want the address?"

"Yeah, sure."

"It's The Rosemount Home on 29 Eden Avenue, Brookline. Orville, no wonder people don't like moving into nursing homes. They all have such lame names." We both laughed.

"What about Roger F. Potter, Jr.?"

"I couldn't find anything on him or that Andrew MacNichol guy. The only thing I found on MacNichol was that an Albert and Lisa MacNichol lived on Belltown Avenue. Albert died in 1966 and Lisa died in 1968."

"Those were his parents. How about Jack Pervis?"

"Yeah. He was reported missing in 1987. He owned a house that his sister Margie lives in, in the summer."

"So it's empty in the winter?" I asked.

"Well, it's listed for rent at Dean's Real Estate. But, who rents just for the winter in Belltown? I figure she'll have a tough time finding someone to rent it."

"How do you find all this stuff out?" I asked in amazement.

"I didn't skip Mr. Allieta's computer class in the eighth grade like someone else I know."

"Guilty as charged." I laughed. "Now where is Jack Pervis's house?"

"Before I answer that, what's this all about?"

"I'm only going to tell you face-to-face, and since there's so much snow on the road . . ."

"My truck has four-wheel drive. I can drive in anything."

"You are different, Gina. You love disco, you're a computer nerd, and you drive a four-wheel drive truck. You should be living in another time period."

"Don't forget my CB, good buddy."

"All right, come over, and I'll tell you the whole story. Now what's Pervis's address?" I gave in.

"Groovy. Jack Pervis's house is on 9 Mayflower

Court. I'll be over in a half hour."

"Thanks again, Gina." I was about to hang up when I thought of something. "Gina, wait."

"Yeah, Orville."

"When was Jack Pervis reported missing in 1987?"

"June 10, 1987."

"When did Ben Beale die?"

"June 18, 1987."

"Wow. That's pretty coincidental. Don't you think?"

"I don't know 'cause I don't know what's going on. Ask me that question in a half hour. Later." She hung up.

My gut told me it was not coincidental. It was murder.

CHAPTER
SEVEN

MY COLD HAD cleared up but my head was still clogged, clogged with thoughts about the case. I couldn't even enjoy the game. Not that there was much to enjoy. Belltown was a heavy favorite, but the snow on the field made it anybody's game. It turned out to be Baywood's when Craig Hampton fumbled on Baywood's three-yard line with eight seconds left in the game. Final score: Baywood 6, Belltown 0. I know you might not believe it, but I really did feel sorry for The Mayor. I may have hated him, but I never like to see the blame put on one player. I don't know. Well anyway, during the game, all I thought about was the case. I had a theory and I worked it in my head. I know, I know, me and my theories, but this one really felt right.

Mrs. Mahoney, *a.k.a.* Audrey Baxter, told me she talked to Jack Pervis about Katherine the day before he disappeared. He told her that he was getting close to the truth.

That meant he must've talked to other people involved in the case, for example, Ben and Justine Beale. Maybe Ben Beale couldn't live with his secret anymore and told Pervis why he changed his testimony. The killer must've found out, and, bang, took care of Jack Pervis and a week later, Ben Beale. But, why didn't he kill Justine Beale, since she changed her testimony, too? I knew I had to go see her soon.

Luckily, Wednesday was an in-service day, which meant a half day, so I could catch a bus to Boston at noon, get my, information, and be home for dinner. I figured I should also take a look at Jack Pervis's house and see if there were any clues still lying around. I knew it was a long shot, but a shot's a shot. What really bothered me was where Andrew MacNichol was. Was he still alive? If he was the killer, he might care if the truth came out, but would he care enough to kill? After all, you can't try someone for the same crime twice. Why would he risk going to prison when he knew the law really couldn't touch him? Maybe he wasn't the killer. If my theory was right and these little pieces of the puzzle fit, 1987 wasn't *that* long ago, I thought.

The killer could still be in Belltown and could be watching every move I make, I thought. After that revelation, I was glad I hadn't told Gina. I had lied, saying I'd give the addresses to Shane so he could look into the case. I decided to put the case out of my head for the rest of the day. I would enjoy the Homecoming Dance with Maria, and then the next day I would get back on the case. I would finally face Will, apologize to him, and then take a peek in Jack Pervis's house.

I couldn't have written a better script. Maria, the girl of my dreams, stood across the gym in a white dress wearing a maroon sash that read "Homecoming Queen." The only lights on were soft strobe lights. A circle of light caught Mr. Finn in the middle of the dance floor with a portable microphone.

Mr. Finn made a few jokes about the game and congratulated the players on their efforts. Then he announced, "It is traditional to begin our Homecoming Dance by having the King and Queen dance the first dance. So, would Orville Jacques and Maria Simpkins please come out here, and everyone else will follow."

I don't know how my feet took me to the middle of the dance floor. I was so nervous, my legs felt like I was walking in quicksand. She put her hands around my shoulders. When I realized how badly I was shaking, I was really showing my school spirit because I turned the school's maroon color.

"Are you nervous?" she whispered in my ear as the music began and we were somehow moving.

"No, why?" I was going to try to fool her even if I couldn't.

"Because I am." Her voice actually trembled.

"Well, actually, me, too," I whispered back in her ear and we both laughed.

"But, *you* shouldn't be," I blurted out.

"Why not? Everyone's watching us." She looked into my eyes.

"Because. . ." I looked away for a second out of embarassment. I was going to continue. I was going to finally Maria how beautiful she was and how much she meant to me, when I was distracted.

"Because. . ." Maria repeated. But, for the first time since I saw her, even Maria couldn't keep my attention. Dr. Harris was talking to Mr. Finn, and he pointed over to Maria and me just as all the other couples joined us on dance floor. What was Dr. Harris doing at the dance? I thought. Then I knew: It meant trouble.

"I'm sorry, Maria. I have to stop. There is something that's wrong." I didn't have time to explain. I dodged the couples on the dance floor and ran to Mr. Finn and Dr. Harris. Dr. Harris's eyes were swollen. I knew she had been crying.

"What is it? Is it Will? Is Will all right?" I yelled.

"Will's in the hospital," Dr. Harris said.

"Oh, my God! What happened?"

"He collapsed this morning. He has severe pneumonia."

"Is he going to be OK?" I said rocking back and forth. "I don't know, honey. Dr. Alden says it doesn't look good." Her voice shook and she hugged me.

"I didn't want to interrupt your dance, but he's been calling your name in his sleep."

"Oh, no!" I must've said that about ten times, then I finally said, "Let's go. Let's go. He can't die! He can't die . . ."

Dr. Alden described Will's condition using words that were absolutely foreign to me.

"So what does all that mean?" I pressed for an answer while watching Will sleep as I looked through the window on the door to his room.

"It means Mr. Michaels has a five percent chance of recovery. He is dying, Orville, and he could pass on at any time," Dr. Alden said matter-of-factly.

"Oh, no. No. He can't die." I was choking on my pain.

"I'm sorry, Orville," Dr. Alden said flatly.

After a minute of silence, Dr. Alden continued, "There is really nothing I can do for him at this stage except provide him with some comfort. You see, he was already sick and then the exposure to the cold weather for that long a time . . ."

"What do you mean?" I asked.

"Jacob Haggerty found Mr. Michaels today on Cranberry Beach. He must've collapsed taking a walk and, judging from his condition, he was on the beach for several hours. It's amazing he made it this long."

"Oh, Will . . ." The thought of Will lying in the snow on Cranberry Beach made the lump in my throat unbearable.

"Can I . . . Can I see him?" I was trying to stay strong.

"Well . . ." he paused, "OK."

Before he could get the word out of his mouth, I was at Will's bedside. Will's eyes were closed and there is no other way to describe it—he looked like he was dying. I slowly took his skeletonlike hand and held it.

"Please, God, take care of him. Let him know how sorry I am for not believing him," I said out loud while looking up to the ceiling.

"I know," Will coughed hard. "You are."

"Will, you're awake." I looked down at Will and his eyes were barely open. He half nodded.

"Will, I'm so sorry. I just wanted to find out the truth for you and Katherine." I was talking a mile a minute.

"I know. I forgave you when you walked out the door," he said slowly.

"You did? Will . . ."

"Orville," he said with all the strength he could muster.

"Yes."

"The doctor said I'm not supposed to talk. But I have a few things to say before I go." He coughed for about ten seconds. It was a heavy cough.

"Don't talk that way," I pleaded.

"It might take me a little while to get it out, so bear with me."

I just nodded.

"I forgave you because you did what I taught you. You were looking for the truth, and you didn't even let our friendship cloud that search. Have you found anything?"

"Bits and pieces." I couldn't tell him that the woman he loved had changed her identity before she met him.

"Good." He smiled weakly. "I want you to keep me updated. I believe you might be able to find out what I couldn't. I have to know."

"OK," I said, and Will must've known what I was thinking.

"I'm not going to die, yet. So, get out of here and let me get some rest."

I managed to smile and then nodded and walked out of the room. I knew Will was dying, but also I believed what he had said. He was not going to die, yet. Something came over me when I walked out of his room. I had to find out the truth for Will, and I would do it no matter what the price was ...

I wasn't going to kid myself into believing Will was going to live much longer, and I wasn't going to waste my energy on false hope. I also wasn't going to waste it on grieving. I knew there would be plenty of time for that later. What I was going to do was put all my energy into the case—and that meant cutting school. I had a lot of work to do.

My first stop was Bill's Donuts. All the old locals went there every morning to talk about last night's game or town politics. I knew if I let them know what I was up to, the killer would hear about it if he was still in town. Then, he'd come to me. I knew I might soon be facing trouble, but I had to find the truth for Will before it was too late. I also hoped someone in town knew where Andrew MacNichol was living—if he was still alive. Bill's Donuts was my answer.

I walked into Bill's, and there were a bunch of the oldtimers hanging out. Today's topic was the new chief of police in Belltown. Some of the locals hated him because he wasn't born and bred in Belltown. Therefore, he wasn't obligated to anyone, so no special favors like fixing tickets. All I know was while *they* were drinking coffee and complaining, the chief was cutting down on crime. The chief's main man was Shane O'Connell and everyone knew I was friends with Shane, so when they spotted me, Bill's Donuts became completely silent.

"Shouldn't you be in school, Orville?" Bill, the owner scowled. He knew I was bad for business. The locals couldn't vent if I hung out there.

"Yeah, I'm on my way. I just wanted to get a honey-dipped doughnut and a hot chocolate."

"Anything else?" he asked, frustrated, watching a couple of the customers head toward the door.

"Actually, yeah, I guess you guys know I like playing kid detective." The locals gave me their attention, dumbfounded.

"Well," I continued, "I've been looking into a case that you guys never seem to talk about."

"What are you talking about, kid?" A few of them grunted.

"I am talking about Katherine Stinson. She was murdered in 1946. They tried to prosecute a guy named

Andrew MacNichol but he was found innocent. Does anyone know where he is now?" I looked around the room. No one answered.

"Well, you might want to tell Mr. MacNichol that I have found out some information that might be very beneficial to him." I was bluffing. I knew if MacNichol was the killer, he'd look for me. If he wasn't the killer, whoever the killer was would figure I must know something that would clear Andrew MacNichol's name. And, of course, he would look for me. By letting the locals at Bill's Donuts in on my search for the truth, I was letting the whole town in. It was better than putting it in the paper.

"That's $1.80," Bill ordered as he put his hand out. I gave him exact change and then turned back to the group who was still trying to make sense of my behavior.

"Thanks, guys. Oh, you can get back to bad-mouthing the chief. Have a nice day."

I took a bite of my honey-dipped doughnut and raised it to Bill and said, "awesome," and headed for the door. Word was out that I was looking into the case, and if the killer was still around I would definitely have to watch my back.

As I approached Jack Pervis's house, I swallowed the last drop of hot chocolate. The walk and driveway hadn't been shoveled. It was a sure sign the house hadn't been rented. I stepped quickly in and out of the snow that had become icy after a few days on the ground. If I had to pick a house to break into, Jack Pervis's was the perfect choice. It was situated far back in the woods on a dead-end street. There was no way I could get caught unless the house had an alarm. I smashed the back window with the hammer I'd brought in my backpack.

I opened the door, which led to the kitchen. I really didn't know what I was looking for, but I knew whatever it was, it certainly wasn't in the kitchen. I went into the living room and picked up the family photo album. I spotted Jack in a picture with his sister and parents. I thought of his poor parents. Their only son had disappeared without a trace. They probably went through the same thing Will went through every night, never knowing the truth. I placed the album down just as I had found it.

I headed upstairs, which, as in most Cape summer houses, was used for storage. I opened a big box that read in black magic marker: Jack's Memories. In the box was everything from a kindergarten picture of Jack and of his high school baseball career and of his articles for the *Cape Cod Times.* I picked up the scrapbook of *Cape Cod Times* articles and walked over under the ceiling light. The light was weak, but I was still able to read. There were all sorts of articles, about Little League games, the Belltown County Fair, movies, local elections, school events, and so on. I realized everything in the scrapbook went by date. I could see the more experience he got, the tougher assignments he wrote about. Then it hit me. I flipped through the scrapbook until I came to

June 6, 1987. It was the last clipping. Headline: Manner Begins Campaign for One More Term. The article was all about Congressman Niles Manner who was from Belltown, Cape Cod. It read:

> Congressman Niles Manner, who has been in office since 1954, has decided he will give it one more go for another term. He will run for reelection against Republican James Thompson from Baywood in November.

The article went on to give a brief history of both candidates, and it ended by stating:

> This is the first article of a series that will spotlight the two candidates' careers showing the pros and cons of each, so the citizens on Cape Cod can make a well-informed decision on Election Day.

I shut the scrapbook and looked straight ahead, thinking.

Jack Pervis told Mrs. Mahoney, *a.k.a.* Audrey Baxter, that he was close to finding the truth. Maybe the truth had something to do with one of the candidates? Maybe he uncovered something about Niles Manner or James Thompson that had something to do with Katherine. There were too many maybe's but if he did find something out about one of the candidates, it would've had to have been Jim Thompson. After all, Niles Manner had been in office for years, there was no way he could have kept any secrets from the public for that long. I had that tingling uneasy feeling I get when there is something that bothers me, and I can't quite put a finger on it. I tried to forget about it as I went to turn the light off. There was a shadow on the side of the wall. It made me jump a bit, but then I realized it was not a human shadow. It was an outline of something. I looked above me. Then I realized why the light was so weak—There was something in it. I grabbed an old rocking chair and got on it, trying to maintain my balance and, at the same time, reaching inside the cover of the light. The chair swayed back and forth as I put my hand into the glass dish covering the ceiling light and felt for the object. I found it the hard way as I grabbed it; a sudden wave of heat ran through my hand and halfway up my arm. I threw it into the air, from the numbing pain, and I fell backward to the floor.

After several seconds, I got up and searched the floor for the object. There it was, right at my feet. It was a key. The bulb must've made the metal hot, I thought. I touched the key quickly. It had cooled down a bit, so I picked it up. I studied it and saw there was a number on it: 127. A key doesn't just get wedged in an attic light by mistake, I thought. Someone put it there. Someone who didn't want anyone to find it. I knew positively that someone was Jack Pervis, and I also knew I had just found another piece to the puzzle ...

Around 2:30 I came home, pretending I was just getting in from school. My mom suggested that we get a few of Will's things and bring them to the hospital, so

he would feel more at home. I brought him his felt hat, his shoe box of letters, his record player and his old records. Will was sleeping, so I set everything up and crept out.

I was going to have to skip school. But my mom and dad would understand. When I got home, I called Dean's Real Estate and disguised my voice. I told them there was a broken window on 9 Mayflower Court. Then I hung up. I knew they would check the house, and then they would find the note I had written:

> We are sorry we broke the window by mis-
> take playing football. I hope the $25.00 will be
> enough for the damages. Thanks.

Of course, I didn't sign a name. I had two reasons for writing the note and leaving the money. One, it was the only decent thing to do after breaking into the house. Two, if I had just left the money and no note, or if I had done nothing, the real estate people may have assumed that someone broke into the house and dropped the money. Then they would have had to file a report and that would have been in the paper. I wanted the killer to know I was looking for him, but I didn't want him to know exactly what I knew. The real estate agent would read the note and realize it was just some scared kids playing where they shouldn't have been playing.

Around 4:00, I decided to give Shane a call. I figured he had probably found out about my visit to Bill's Donuts. I got his answering machine. "Hi, you've reached Detective Shane O'Connell's office, and I am not here right now. I am away for a few days on police business ..." I hung the phone up. I don't know if I was relieved to find out he was away or not. I kind of wanted him to know what was going on because I didn't really know where to go next. I decided to take a walk on Cranberry Beach and think of everything that had happened the past few days. I put on my Walkman and turned the dial to 92.7 WMVY. It was the Vineyard station and sometimes it would give me a much-needed taste of the summer. My instincts were right because when I approached Cranberry Beach, the D.J. said, "Now a double shot of two of the Cape's best bands. We'll kick off with Johnny Hoy and The Bluefish and then some Entrain so you can dream about cookouts and warm summer night walks on the beach. Hang in there folks, summer isn't that far away."

"Yeah, right." I laughed as I turned it up and hummed along to Johnny Hoy's bluesy voice while walking through the sandy snow. Summer was so far away, I thought but then my thoughts shifted to Will and Katherine, Andrew MacNichol, Jack Pervis, Niles Manner, James Thompson, and the key.

The pink sun was falling asleep in the sea, and it was getting dark. I realized my next visit would have to be to Justine Beale at The Rosemount Home. "She has to have some answers," I said out loud. I would have to take the first bus to Boston in the morning. I knew in a couple of days I would be found out, and I would pay the price. But I thought this was more important than Mr. Reasons's talks on finding the meaning of x.

I decided to just enjoy the last song which was one of my favorite Entrain songs, "Dancin' In The Light."I hummed away and sang parts of the song I knew and instantly warmed up during the driving drum solo.When the song ended, the D.J. cut to a commercial, so I reached into my coat pocket and turned off my Walkman. In the silence, I heard footsteps. There was someone behind me, gaining on me. I tried not to let my fright show. I pretended I was still listening to my Walkman, humming away. I heard the person say, "Hey," to see if I would respond. I just kept humming.

"Can't hear me, huh?" the voice said with an evil laugh.

I knew I was in trouble. I had one thing on my side though—he thought I couldn't hear him behind me, so he was taking his time. He was enjoying it. I sensed he was about three feet behind me. I tried desperately to keep humming. When I heard him say, "This is going to be fun," I didn't even hesitate. I turned in an instant and gave him a kick with my boots in the only place that would guarantee pain. I watched his face for a split second. It was a face of pain and disbelief at the same time. I ran as hard as I could as he lay for a few moments on the beach, writhing in pain. Then I heard him yell, "I'm going to get you, you little ..."

My head start meant nothing. He was gaining on me. In the split second I had seen him, I knew he was trouble—he was blond, athletic looking, in his early thirties. I was gulping for breath as I came to the steps of the beach wall. Trying to run up the steps, I slipped and fell to the ground. The man stood over me, laughing.

"Nice try, kid. But, did you really think you were going to get away from me?" He picked me up with one hand. I didn't say anything. I couldn't. I knew he was planning to really make me pay for kicking him.

"You know, that was pretty stupid of you today at the doughnut shop. I mean, my boss knew you were looking into the murder, but he was going to let it go. He knew you would never find the truth. But, you had to let everyone know you were looking." He slapped me with his right hand. My face felt like it had been stung by a thousand bees. I tried to control my quivering lip.

The man continued, "It's old news, but you had to put it back into people's heads, and now maybe that loser cop friend of yours, O'Connell, might start asking questions. So before this goes any further, he told me that I'm supposed to take care of you."

"Can I ask . . . who . . . he is?" I managed.

"Kid, you can ask all you want." He laughed. "Now, come with me." He grabbed my hand and was about to put some handcuffs on me when a voice behind us yelled, "Leave him alone. Now!"

We both looked behind us, and Mr. Haggerty stood there holding his metal detector.

"Leave us alone, old man. This is between him and me."

"That kid, as you say, happens to be a friend of mine."

The guy let go of me and walked over to Mr. Haggerty. "What if I don't want to leave him alone? What are you going to do?" The man went face-to-face with

Mr. Haggerty, but he didn't back down.

"What am I going to do? I guess I would be going to your funeral, young fellow. Now you wouldn't want that to happen, would you?"

Mr. Haggerty pulled a gun out of his winter coat pocket and pointed it at the man, who was in complete shock that Mr. Haggerty was packing a piece. I couldn't believe it myself! The guy looked over at me and whispered, "This ain't over, kid," then bolted down the beach.

"What is going on, Orville?" Mr. Haggerty asked, patting me on the back. I couldn't involve him, so I knew I had to lie.

"I was in a fight with his brother, and he was kind of paying me back."

"It looked like more to me than that."

"No, he's just mad 'cause I embarrassed his brother."

"Well, you're shaking like a leaf. You really should tell someone." He put the gun back in his jacket.

"I will. Thanks so much Mr. Haggerty."

"No problem."

"Why do you carry a gun, though?" I still couldn't believe this old man packed a piece.

"It's my old .45 automatic from the Korean War. One of these days, I figure I'm going to find something of real value with this detector, and I want to be sure I keep it."

That thinking was a little paranoid, but who was I to criticize him?

"Orville, your nose is bleeding. Why don't you come to my house and clean up? You don't want your parents to see that."

"Yeah," I agreed.

"And I can also show you my metal detector collection." He smiled.

"Yeah, that would be nice." I smiled. I really didn't have time to look at a bunch of old metal, but I wasn't going to talk my way out of it. I owed Mr. Haggerty at least fifteen minutes of my time, if not my life . . .

CHAPTER
EIGHT

I CLEANED UP my face in Mr. Haggerty's bathroom. I stared into the mirror for a while. What if Mr. Haggerty hadn't come along? As I wiped the last of the blood off my lip, I said to myself, What did you get yourself into this time? I had to get in touch with Shane soon, but first I had to hang out with Mr. Haggerty. I owed him. I went back into the sitting room, which had a warm, coal-stove fire going. Mr. Haggerty came out of the kitchen with a tray and put it on the table.

"Oh, Mr. Haggerty. I really just want to see your metal detector collection and then I better get going. It's getting late."

"Nonsense, Orville. You have time for a bowl of my famous clam chowder." He offered me a bowl.

"My parents . . ." I began.

"I called your parents and told them we met on the beach, and you were going to have dinner with me, and your dad said he would pick you up in an hour."

"Oh, OK." I was glad I accepted, too, because it was probably the best bowl of clam chowder I ever had. That says a lot since Cape Cod is known for its chowder. After we ate, he brought me into the den. As he went into his desk to look for something, I stared at the pictures on the wall.

There was one of a young man in an army uniform. He was probably two years older than me at the most.

"That's my son. Raymond. I called him Ray Ray."

"How old was he when he . . . died?" I don't know why I asked. Maybe because he wasn't that much older than me, and the scene on the beach was scaring me.

"They never found Ray Ray's body. So part of me still likes to think he's alive." Mr. Haggerty paused for a second and then dropped the subject.

"Now, Orville. Check this out." He handed me a photo album. I opened it expecting pictures, but saw coins. "I have coins in there from all over the world, China, Ireland, Germany, check this one out." He pointed enthusiastically.

"Peru," I said.

"Yup, Peru. I also have found pins and medals. Look at this one." He pointed.

"What is it?" I looked at a medal that had some Chinese characters or something on it.

"That's a medal that's given to kids in China after they pass a swimming test." He smiled.

"How do you know that?"

"Research. I research everything I find. Even the spoons. I found a spoon that was from the early 1800s. Here, I'll show you." He put down the photo album, and we walked over to the other side of the room where he had all the bigger metal objects on a table with a description on an index card. I looked at the descriptions, and there was the spoon. There was also a metal pail dated 1910 and a washboard dated 1860.

"I know you do research, but how are you certain of the dates?" I was interested. My fear had almost left me.

"Well, what I don't know, I ask the professionals and they date it for me." He kept talking, but one of the objects caught my eye and I was only half listening.

"I eventually would like to open a small museum. I'd call it Cranberry Beach Treasures or Cranberry Beach Museum. Which one do you think?" he asked. I was still reading the description of the object that caught my eye.

"The second one," I said, but I really hadn't heard him because I was too baffled at what I had read. Finally, I read it out loud. "Door handle of a 1945 Ford Beach Wagon."

"What, Orville?"

"This says that this rusty thing is a door handle of a 1945 Ford Beach Wagon. How do you know that, Mr. Haggerty?" I almost shouted.

"Just as I told you. I did research. Why?" He looked at me wondering at my excitement.

"Are you positive?" I asked.

"Of course I'm positive. Why are you acting so strange? You know," he said, snapping his fingers, you're the second person to act like that when he saw the door handle."

Mr. Haggerty was trying to figure out what my problem was. I didn't answer his question. I just asked, "Who was the first person?"

"Well, you probably wouldn't remember him. His name was Jack Pervis. He was a reporter for the *Cape Cod Times.*"

"Jack Pervis saw your collection?" I was trying to calm down, but the adrenaline was pumping.

"Yes. I used to see Jack taking walks on Cranberry Beach like you. I figured since he wrote for the *Cape Cod Times,* he might want to do an article on my collection. Of course, that was back in 1987, and it wasn't as big as it is now. Well, anyway, Jack came by the house and looked at my collection, and he was remarkably interested in my 1945 Ford Beach Wagon door handle."

"Why do you say remarkably interested?"

"Well, he kept asking me if I were sure that was the make of the door handle. I told him that I knew it was because I knew cars, having been in the business for years, and another thing I had looked it up in my books. Well, that wasn't enough for him. He wanted a second opinion, and he said he'd pay for it. So I went all the way to Boston to find out. Sure enough, I was right. But, I couldn't tell Jack because he disappeared. They never did find him. His poor parents—I know how they feel."

He shook his head. He did know how they felt.

I couldn't believe my good fortune, and my dad couldn't have had better timing. The doorbell rang and saved me from thinking up some lie about why I was so interested in a car door handle from 1945. I thanked Mr. Haggerty and on my way out the door said, "Cranberry Beach's Hidden Treasures."

"What?" He looked puzzled.

"For a name for your museum. Cranberry Beach's Hidden Treasures."

"Hidden Treasures. I like that!" He smiled.

There was no question in my mind that the door handle was the greatest treasure of them all and opened a treasure chest of clues . . .

I sprinted up the stairs to my room and pulled out the KATHERINE STINSON, MURDER CASE #0231 folder from between my bed mattress and box spring. I opened it and pulled out my notes. I read them over and over again.

I reviewed Roger Potter's explanation of how the door handle had broken off. When I got to the part that read, "There was scattered laughter in the courtroom," I stopped, shaking my head. This guy went up on the stand and lied. He did it so well that people actually laughed at the idea that these questions were being asked. Roger F. Potter, Jr., was a liar under oath. That meant he knew what really happened. Where was he now? I had to find him.

I put my notes away and was about to call it a night when I realized something that I didn't even bother to write down in my notes about Roger F. Potter, Jr. I didn't think it would matter much. I knew now it did. I looked for the excerpt of State Trooper Roger F. Potter's testimony.

> My name is Roger F. Potter, Jr. My badge number is 566. I am a state trooper for the Commonwealth of Massachusetts.

"Badge number 566. 566. 566. 566." I said it over and over again. The number seemed so familiar to me and then it hit me, the retired policeman at the governor's dinner wore his old shield. The number on the shield was 566.

"Oh, my God!" I gasped. The man who told me that Will was a dirty cop was Roger F. Potter, Jr. I was pumped when it all came to me. I finally had a face to look for. But, it also angered me. I had taken this stranger's word about my good friend, and it turned out that he was involved in this crime. I had the proof. I knew it was nothing that could probably stand up in court. But, it was concrete evidence for my own mind. Roger F. Potter, Jr. was involved in Katherine Stinson's murder. I was going to find the concrete proof, and as I finally settled into bed the last words I mumbled were, "You shouldn't have opened your big mouth State Trooper Potter 'cause I'm gonna get you!"

I slipped out of my house at 6:02 AM. I knew if the blond guy was watching my house, he wouldn't come by that early, considering I usually left for school at 7:20. I crept out the back door just in case and scanned the front yard to make sure the coast was clear. Sunrise wasn't for at least another hour, but the sky in the east was getting light. There were no signs of cars or people, and I was fairly confident I was safe.

I had to call Shane, but I still was not sure that he was back from police business, so I decided I would go ahead with my plan. My plan was to take the 6:30 AM bus to Boston's Back Bay Station. Then, take the *T*—Boston's equivalent of a subway to Brookline, where I would head to The Rosemount Home, find Justine Beale, and ask her why she had changed her testimony. If she didn't answer me, I would tell her about the evidence and refuse to leave unless she answered my questions. Then, I would call Shane and he could take over from there.

The bus ride took an hour and a half, and I have to admit, I was glad to have some time to think. There were all sorts of people on the bus but luckily no one I knew. Since no one took the seat next to me, I stretched my legs on the other seat and relaxed. I reflected on everything from Will's health to the last time I had seen Maria. I had left her on the dance floor. I was going to tell her what she meant to me but then the distraction. I knew the next time I saw her I wouldn't even hesitate. I would tell her my feelings. The whole ordeal with Will's almost dying before I could apologize had taught me a valuable lesson. Life goes by too quickly and it's a waste if you don't resolve conflicts or tell the people what they mean to you. I had spent so much time playing mind games with Maria. I had to tell her the truth, and if she didn't feel the same way about me, even though it would hurt, I would at least be able to live with myself. As Will said, "Not knowing the truth is paralyzing."

When I finished thinking about Maria, I put my mind back on the case. I pulled out of my coat pocket the key I had found at Jack Pervis's house—127. What lock did it fit? I mused. It may have nothing to do with the case, but I had a gut feeling it did. I looked closer at the key and saw something I hadn't noticed before. There were three tiny initials on the key: *B.B.&T.*

B.B.&T. What does *B.B.&T.* stand for? I asked myself. Belltown Bank & Trust. "That's it!" I sat up in my seat and then realized people were staring at me. I sat back in my seat and studied the key. If I was right, there was only one thing the key could unlock—a safe deposit box. Inside the safe deposit box could be the answers that I was looking for.

When the bus arrived at the Back Bay Station, I almost didn't want to get off. I wanted to go straight back to Belltown and see what was in the safe deposit box. I wondered if it were Jack Pervis's box or someone else's. When I got back to Belltown, I knew I could call Gina, and she would probably be able to find out exactly whose box it was by the number on the key and some of her clever computer work.

On the *T,* it was standing room only until the fourth

stop, when some of the business types got off I still had a long way to go, so I was pretty psyched to grab a seat. I tried to zone out for a while, but I had the strange sense that somebody was watching me. I knew it was probably paranoia. But, then again, I had every reason to be paranoid. I thought of what the blond-haired guy had said, "My boss ..." Boss. What if the blond-haired guy wasn't the only person hired to get me? I tried to stay calm, but I felt a panic attack coming on. The more I tried not to think that way, the more I felt eyes on me. Of course, there were eyes on me. People were facing me and naturally were staring straight ahead. But as I was beginning to chalk up my paranoia to my imagination, I suddenly noticed one particular pair of eyes. They stood out among the sea of blank expressions. The eyes would glance over at me at each stop to see if I would get off. He was probably in his early thirties. He wore a Boston Red Sox hat, an L.L. Bean barn jacket, and a pair of faded jeans. He had jet-black hair and a perfectly trimmed mustache. His eyes met mine and they locked for a second until I finally managed to look away. A few seconds passed, and then a sneeze came from his direction. Curiosity was killing me. I wanted to check and see who sneezed. I turned. It was the man with the Red Sox hat. Something about him seemed so familiar, but I couldn't place it. He wiped his nose with his handkerchief and glanced at me again as we approached the next stop. When he took the handkerchief from his nose, I noticed something about that perfectly trimmed mustache. It wasn't so perfect. In fact, it was a little askew.

Not much, but just enough for me to realize it was not real. He was wearing a fake mustache. The man put his finger on it to fix it and then stared over at me. My head was telling my eyes to look away but they didn't listen. Our eyes locked again and this time I placed him. I knew. He gave a slow and deliberate nod while smiling to let me know he knew I knew. It was the blond-haired man from Cranberry Beach except now he had jet-black hair and a fake mustache. A muffled voice on the intercom announced the stop. The doors swished. I was trying to stay in control but when he got up out of his seat and headed toward me, I thought I was going to faint. I couldn't think of a plan, so I figured acting on impulse was probably my best chance for escape. Just as the doors were shutting, I leaped out of my seat and jumped through them, and they closed behind me. I turned around and saw the man punching the door in frustration as the *T* rocked back and forth, then flew off down the tracks.

I smiled in relief. The relief lasted only a brief second. This was no game. The man had dyed his hair and put on a fake mustache and followed me to Boston. I was in major danger, and I had to cancel my trip to The Rosemount Home. If he knew everything else, he probably figured I was headed there. I had to make it back to the Back Bay Station before he caught up to me. There I could jump on the bus back to Belltown. I jumped on the *T* headed to Back Bay Station. I knew I had at least a fifteen-minute head start, considering he was heading the other way. I was breathing hard when I got to Back

Bay. I went to buy my ticket for the bus to Belltown, and the clerk informed me the next bus wasn't till 10:00. It was 9:15. He would have caught me by then. I spotted a row of phones and ran over and dialed Shane's number. It seemed like hours before it finally rang.

"Please pick up! Pick up, Shane!" I shouted.

"Hi . . ."

"Shane!"

. . . you've reached Detective Shane O'Connell's office, and I am not here right now . . ."

I slammed the phone on the receiver.

"Who can I call up here? Mark? But he lives in Framingham. That's at least a half hour away." Mark was my summer friend, and he lived in a suburb west of Boston. He was the only person I knew who lived off Cape.

"Think!" I was running out of time. Then it came to me. I pulled out my wallet and searched for the card frantically. "Ryan Kane. Celebration Limousine." I pegged the number and breathed, "Please, God, let him be there."

"Hello," a voice said quickly.

"Yes, is this Ryan Kane?"

"Ah, no. Let me check and see if he's in." I could hear the voice yell, "Ryan here yet?"

A couple of seconds passed but it seemed to take forever as I watched a *T* approach.

"Hello, Ryan Kane at your service."

"Ryan, hi, this is Orville Jacques. Remember me? You drove us in the limo to the governor's dinner." I spoke quickly into the phone while watching people get off the *T*.

"Yeah, Orville. Is something wrong? You sound up-set."

"I am. I can't explain but I need help. I'm being followed!"

"OK. Calm down. Now where are you?"

"Back Bay Station. Oh, my God! There he is!" I spot-ted him getting off the *T*.

"Does he see you?" Ryan asked calmly.

"Not yet! What do I do?" The man wearing the Red Sox cap was looking around Back Bay Station.

"Kozens Bakery is two streets up from the Back Bay Station. I want you to go there. I'll call Frannie and she'll be waiting for you. I'll be there in ten minutes."

"Oh, my God! He sees me!" At that moment the man began running up the stairs.

"Kozens Bakery." I banged the phone down and sprinted out the door, took a right, and headed up two streets. It took me about five minutes until I saw the sign. I looked behind me and there was no sign of him, so I ducked inside.

"Orville?" A woman rushed from behind the counter.

I just nodded, gasping for breath.

"Ryan will be here shortly. Come with me." She turned to a young girl. "Watch the counter."

Frannie showed me through the back kitchen and pointed up a stairwell.

"You can hide up in my house until Ryan gets here."

"Thank you." How lucky could I get?

I went up the stairs and sat on her couch, trying to gain my composure. My lungs ached, and I was shaking uncontrollably. No question about it, I was petrified. After about ten minutes, my breathing was getting back to normal. I heard footsteps on the stairs and Ryan Kane stood right before me. We skipped the greetings.

"Was he wearing a Red Sox baseball cap?" Ryan asked.

"Yeah. How did you know?" I asked, as we shook hands.

"Frannie said some guy came into the bakery wearing a Sox cap and described you. He said you stole his wallet and ran this way."

"Stole his wallet?" I shook my head.

"Frannie covered perfect." He laughed. "She said no wonder you wanted to hide in the bakery. She figured you must've done something wrong, so she kicked you out and you kept running up the street."

"What did the guy say?" I propped up in the couch.

"Nothing. He just ran out the door and headed up the street."

"Thank God." I meant every word.

"Now what's going on?" Ryan sat beside me.

"How long do you have?" I managed to smile.

"As long as it takes." He smiled back.

After I had finished telling Ryan my story, he insisted on driving me back to Belltown in his limo. And there was no way I was going to turn down the offer. He parked the limo in the back alley once he thought it was safe, sent Frannie to get me. I jumped in the passenger seat, and we buzzed onto the main road.

"Wherever that guy is looking for you, I can almost guarantee you it's not in a limo." He laughed and I joined him.

After Ryan dropped me off, I called Shane, as I'd promised Ryan I would. Ryan had become a loyal friend quickly, and I knew how fortunate I had been to have him help me. If not? Well, I don't even want to think about that.

When I dialed Shane's number, I got his machine. I left a calm message: "Shane, Orville here. I've found some major stuff about the K.S. case. Call me. Urgent."

I was starving, so I made a couple of English muffin pizzas and put them in the toaster oven. I called to check on Will and Dr. Alden said, "His status is the same."

Next I called Gina. We talked a little about Will and then I got right to the point.

"I have a key here from the Belltown Bank & Trust."

"Yeah. What do you need to know?"

"It's number 127. I need to know the owner of the key."

"So, we're talking a safe deposit box?"

"Yeah. Can you do it?"

"Now we're talking. That's some serious stuff, Orville. But, I think I can. Give me a half hour or so. Can I ask . . ."

"No, you can't. Thanks G." I hung up before she could even argue. I got all my notes together and put them into my backpack. I figured I should have everything together just in case Shane got back into town and wanted to talk. I even packed my mini tape recorder. I sat at the kitchen table and drank a soda. A few minutes later my mom and dad came in with some groceries.

"Hi, Orville. Could you give us a hand?" My dad said while handing me some bags.

"Sure, I'll put the food away because I'm waiting on a phone call, anyway."

"Who, Maria Simpkins?" My mom said out of the blue.

"Maria? Why would I be waiting on a call from her?"

"Well, she called earlier."

"What?" I said in shock.

"Yes. I left you a message on the kitchen table."

We both looked and couldn't find it, and then I picked up the *Boston Globe* and there it was, underneath. It read:

"4:30. Maria Simpkins called. She's at Coffee Obsession. She'll be there for a couple of hours studying if you want to join her."

It was a little after 5:30 and dark. I knew I should probably stay in my own house where I'd be safe. But, the blond man probably figured I wasn't crazy enough to go out alone after what had happened. He was probably still in Boston, anyway, staking out the bus stop figuring that was my only way home. I decided I would go see Maria at Coffee 0 (that's what everyone called it), after Gina called. The phone finally rang.

"Do you recognize the name Lawrence Thames?"

"Lawrence Thames? No."

"Well, Box 127 was bought by a Lawrence Thames, January 1, 1945."

"I don't know if that means anything to me, but it could mean everything."

"What's really strange, Orville, he bought it for one hundred years. And with most boxes only certain people are allowed to use the key. But, with this one, anyone who has the key is allowed to open the box. I guess he knew he wouldn't be alive to open it himself in a hundred years." She laughed.

"So you're telling me if I went in there tomorrow with my key I could open it?" I felt a chill go up my spine.

"That's right." I could feel her smile on the other line.

"Awesome! Gina I owe you big, but I have to explain later. I'll call you later on."

"OK, Orville, groovy." Gina managed to let it go.

When I hung up, my mind was spinning "Lawrence Thames."

"Lawrence!" I shouted. The man with Katherine that night went by the name of Lawrence. Was this a coincidence or was there really a Lawrence? I had to wait another day. But, that didn't mean this one was over. I was going to Coffee O to find out why Maria wanted my company. I had faced enough fear for one day that I was confident I would be able to confront one of my worst fears—telling her how I felt about her ...

CHAPTER
NINE

THE SUN THAT day had melted most of the snow, but there was still enough on the ground to make it too slick for my bike. I didn't mind though—the fifteen-minute walk to Coffee 0 gave me time to think about the case. Lawrence Thames. Who was Lawrence Thames? What did he have to do with any of this? And how did Jack Pervis get Lawrence Thames's key? The next day those questions might be answered when I opened the box. I couldn't wait!

I thought about Gina and how much she had helped. I couldn't have done it without her. Then it hit me. I hadn't really done anything. I had looked into an unsolved murder, and I had found all these different pieces of a puzzle, but I still had no clue who the real murderer was. It could've been Andrew MacNichol, but he was found innocent. Why would he hire someone to kill me? It just didn't make any sense. I had no solid proof about anything except that Katherine Stinson lied about who she was. And that wasn't much because I still didn't know who she *really* was.

As I approached Coffee 0, it struck me. I did have one piece of proof and that was the door handle. The door handle that Roger F. Potter, Jr., claimed he broke off the night before Katherine Stinson was abducted. I jogged over to the pay phone right beside Coffee 0. I knew State Trooper Roger F. Potter's name. I knew his old badge number—566. I knew what he looked like now. If anyone could get me an address on Potter, Gina could.

She picked up the phone and before she could say "hi" I said, "Gina, are you by your computer?"

"Yeah, I'm upstairs in my room. Why?"

"I have more work for you."

"All right, but where are you? The phone sounds funny."

"I'm at a pay phone outside Coffee O."

"Why are you there?"

"I can't explain. I want you to look up a name for me. Roger F. Potter, Jr."

"Didn't you have me do that before?"

"Badge number 566, Massachusetts State Police."

"I know just where to look."

I didn't say a word, just pumped dimes into the phone.

Finally she said, "Here we go. I got him. There's a lot of information, his bio and stuff, what do you need?"

"When did he become a cop?"

"In 1943 and retired in 1973. He was highly decorated. After he retired . . . wow." She stopped.

"He became a private driver for Congressman Niles Manner."

"Niles Manner!" I screamed into the phone.

"Yeah, Potter drove him until Potter retired in June of 1987."

"June of 1987!"

"Yeah, that's right," she said.

"What was the day?" I demanded.

"It doesn't say."

I had so many questions. "Where does he live?"

"He lives in Boston on . . . oh, my God. . ."

"What, Gina?"

"I just read the bottom of the screen. It says Roger F. Potter died three days ago. He was found in an alley, dead. A victim of a mugging that had gone wrong."

"Or a murder that had gone right!"

"What, Orville?"

"Gina, could you punch up Congressmen Niles Manner?" My heart was about to burst. Pieces of the puzzle were beginning to fit.

"Sure. That's easy. I wish I knew what this was all about. Does it have anything to do with Katherine Stinson?"

"You will know soon enough." I pumped another dime.

"I got him. What do you need on him?"

"What was he doing in June of 1987, like in Congress?" A couple of seconds passed.

"This is pretty interesting, Orville. There was a bill brought up about having a conservation park in Belltown."

"Manner Park. I know it's named after him." I jumped in.

"Yeah, but originally he wasn't for the park because he supported some developers, but, at the last minute, he changed his vote."

"What was the date of his vote?"

"June 15, 1987."

"June 15, 1987?"

"That's what I said."

"Gina you may have just solved ..." I stopped. I saw a black limousine pull up outside the phone booth. Ryan didn't go back to Boston, he was keeping an eye on me, I thought.

"Gina, I gotta go, thanks a lot."

"But, Orville ..."

"Talk to you later, thanks, 'bye." I hung up the phone.

Niles Manner had something to do with Jack Pervis being missing and the murders of Katherine Stinson, Ben Beale and Roger Potter. I knew it. "But why?" I asked myself. My gut told me where Jack Pervis could be found. I walked over to the limo. I was shaking with excitement. I had to go with Ryan and forget about Maria for now. I looked back quickly to see if she was in the coffee shop. I heard the limo door open. I turned, and it wasn't Ryan who got out of the limo.

I knew I was in trouble. I made a desperate attempt to run but he was too close. The blond man grabbed my neck, squeezed it and growled, "Get in the back or I'll break it. And God, do I want to."

He opened the back door with one hand and threw me in with the other. I looked up and saw an old man sitting in the back of the limo. He was tall and strong looking. He was well dressed and had gigantic rings on both fingers. He didn't have to tell me his name. I had seen him in the newspapers and on TV many times.

"Mr. Orville Jacques, I presume." He put out his hand. I shook it. I figured I'd better or else.

"I am Congressman Niles Manner. Or should I say, retired Congressman Niles Manner." He pushed a switch and the dividing window between the driver and the back seat passenger's opened.

"Oh, Jason. I think we'll take the long route this time."

"Yes, sir," the blond/black-haired man said.

"Orville, may I call you Orville?" I nodded yes. "Orville and I have a lot of catching up to do." He pushed the button and the window went up.

"I have to say, Orville you really should feel honored."

"Why do you say that?"

"Not many people get the explanation." He smiled, playing, with one of his rings. My stomach was turning.

"Sir, I don't know what you are talking about. I don't know who that Jason guy is, or why he was chasing me."

I guess I was not convincing because he said, "Orville, please don't insult my intelligence, I didn't insult yours."

"What do you mean?"

"The microfilm in the library."

"Yeah." I gulped. I might as well not play dumb.

"One of my long-time associates saw you looking up the case and he took the microfilm." He stopped and said to himself, "In retrospect, that was probably not a smart thing for him to do. That probably intrigued you more about the case."

"Yes, it did. Who was the associate?" I asked, trying to think who would be on his payroll.

"I suppose you have a right to know. It was Bob Powers."

"Bob Powers!"

"Yes, I believe he coached you in Little League."

I was in shock. Mr. Powers seemed like such a great guy.

"Yes, Bob has worked for me for years, just keeping an eye on things in Belltown."

"What is this all about?" I was scared but curious.

"I will say you are privileged in what I'm about to tell You. Many have tried to find the story and more than many have failed. But, I feel you deserve to know. I will ask you one question before I tell you. Did you figure out I killed Katherine Stinson?" He looked me straight in the eye.

I was horrified. I finally managed, "No, I thought maybe it was State Trooper Potter."

"That's what I thought. You were on the right track. It was only a matter of time. Roger Potter was a major help to me for years. He said he met you at the governors dinner."

"Yes."

"I figured that's what got you so interested in Will Michael's past. It's too bad Roger opened his mouth. I did like Roger. He was always so reliable," he thought aloud.

He was so cool and calm that I was almost strangely relaxed.

"So you killed Potter?"

"Well, if he hadn't talked to you, you wouldn't have looked into the past."

"The past." I repeated the words for him.

"Oh, yes, I did promise you an explanation." He paused.

"I guess I'll begin in Chicago, the winter of 1935. I was just a kid. An orphan without any money or a home. I met a few people on the streets. I began working for a family called Marcirello. They had been associated in the early days with the big names like Al Capone. Am I boring you, Orville?" His tone was a little sharper.

"No, no." I had been looking through the tinted window trying to figure out where he was taking me. When he said the name Capone, I knew that meant mob and that meant I wasn't going to be just roughed up a bit, I was going to be killed. I was trying to think of a plan.

"Well, one night I went with these two other guys to a restaurant called The Silver Swan. We went to get the usual protection money after the place had closed. It was just going to be routine, until the guy who was supposed to give us the money pulled out a gun. He shot one of the guys I was with and then his gun jammed.

So we killed him, and then we found his wife who was hiding in the back room and we made her open the safe. We loaded up all the money and left."

"What about the man's wife?" I couldn't believe I was able to ask questions knowing my time was running out. Maybe that was the answer. Stall.

"She was an eyewitness. Too bad, too, she was a pretty woman. Her daughter was the spitting image of her."

"Daughter?"

"Yes. Margaret Ann Campbell." He paused. "But you would know her as Katherine Stinson."

After I digested this, I asked, "Why did you kill Katherine, I mean Margaret Ann? What did she have to do with her parents?"

"Well, Margaret Ann saw us come in and she hid under a table when she heard the gunshots. The guy I was with—George Parker—was picked up in less than twenty-four hours. When I heard that, I took my cut of the money and left Chicago for the last place I thought people would look, seaside Belltown, Cape Cod. I changed my name, went to law school, and began a career in government. In the back of my mind, though, I knew Margaret Ann Campbell could identify me if she ever saw me. So I hired a friend to track her down. He couldn't find her, but he did find the FBI agent who helped relocate her, Lawrence Thames."

It was hard not to let on that I had heard the name, Lawrence Thames, before. I had his key in my pocket.

"That was before any witness protection programs were really initiated, but Lawrence Thames felt it was his duty to get her protection and a new identity."

"When your friend found him, Lawrence Thames told him where she was."

"No." He shook his head. "Thames was true to his word. He never talked, so instead he took a swim in the river, and I guess he liked the water too much." He laughed.

"Kind of like Ben Beale did in 1987." I glared at him.

"You are good, Orville." He continued, laughing. "Of all the places in the world Margaret Ann picks to relocate, she picks Boston. And of all the places on the Cape she picks to go in the summer, she picks Belltown. Can you believe that? I had only seen her in pictures, but I was positive it was her, Margaret Ann Campbell was at the Belltown Dance Hall. It was just two days after I had someone kill Lawrence Thames in Chicago. To this day, I can't believe my good fortune. What a small world, huh?"

Jason put down the window. "Sir, we're almost there."

"OK, Jason, I'm almost finished. Give me five more minutes."

He pushed the button and the window slid up. I would have to fight soon, but I tried to stay calm. Shane once advised me that in a situation like this, there is always hope if you stay in control.

"Where was I? Oh, yes. I saw Margaret Ann Campbell, and I figured I had to get her before she saw me. That's where Andrew MacNichol came in. His father owed some friends of mine some serious money and favors. All I had to do was have my buddy Potter put a gun to the head of Andrew's mother. That was pretty persuasive."

"How were you friends with Potter?" Now I was definitely stalling.

"Potter was as dirty as they come. That's what I thought was so funny about his comment to you about Will Michaels. I think in his old age, he wanted to believe he was clean like he really earned all those medals. How ironic that he had to die because of that comment. Don't you think?"

"Yes, I guess so."

"Back to MacNichol. He and I went to Cranberry Beach, and I pulled off the door handle in the inside passenger's door. There was no way I wanted her to escape. That was when Ben and Justine Beale spotted us, but I didn't know that at the time. Andrew drove to the dance hall and told Margaret that he was an FBI agent, and Lawrence had called and said there was trouble. She left the dance with him, and he drove her to the bogs. You should have seen the look on her face when she saw me."

"You sick . . ." My blood was boiling.

"Now Orville, let's not ruin such a pleasant chat."

"So you threatened the Beales?" I had to keep asking questions.

"Very easy. Nice people, just wanted to live their own life. And a few dollars in their pocket. Unfortunately, Ben's conscience got to him in 1987. And Justine has had Alzheimer's since before that. Justine just didn't have those memories anymore."

"Why did Potter cover for Andrew MacNichol?"

"I had to save MacNichol because I knew if he went to jail he'd sing. After the trial he disappeared. He knew I was going to take care of him. To this day, I wonder where he is. He's caused me many sleepless nights." He shook his head.

"Why did you set up Will Michaels?"

"Many people in town thought he had killed her, so I decided to make him look like a dirty cop. That way, many people concluded he must've had something to do with the murder. The case was dropped and forgotten until . . ."

"Jack Pervis."

"Yes." He nodded. "I think he was really on to me but then he disappeared. And then that story that Jack Pervis was a drug runner. God, I don't know where I'd be without the small town gossip." He burst into laughter.

The dividing window came down.

"Sir, we're here."

"Perfect timing. Orville, we are . . ."

"You don't have to tell me. Manner Park."

"You are good. I like to call it Manner Garden, though."

His laugh wasn't sane as he reached into his coat pocket.

He pulled out a gun and pointed it at me.

"Too bad we didn't meet under better circumstances. I truly admire your sleuthing ability. Now, get out of the car."

"No, if you're going to kill me, I'm not going to walk to my grave like Jack Pervis."

I lunged for the gun and felt a hand pull me from behind. It was Jason. He grabbed my neck with one hand and slammed a cloth over my mouth. I tried not to inhale, but it was a losing battle. The odor was like ammonia, and things became dizzy. Everything was blurring and I heard Jason say, "Jack Pervis didn't walk to his grave, he was dragged like a dead dog."

Then I heard them both laughing until it became muffled and the blur turned dark, darker, and then black ...

I was drifting in and out of consciousness. Everything was foggy. Sounds seemed faraway, and I couldn't think straight. The foggy feeling slowly cleared, and I woke up.

I put a hand on my head and could feel the blood flowing freely from my brow. I heard an engine for a few seconds, and I was trying to figure out where I was. Was I in a car? I thought. My senses didn't agree with the thought. I heard crashing waves in the distance and a chorus of screaming seagulls. I tried to focus on my surroundings. The sound of the sea and gulls was suddenly drowned out by the roar of an engine. Was I in a boat? I realized I was lying down. And whatever type of engine was rattling was above me. I could see a flash of light. I was still confused. I heard a voice above "Back up a little more. A little more. Good, perfect. You got it."

The engine then died and then silence. I could hear the ocean and sea birds again. I must be near a beach. I thought. I was about to get up when a light shone directly into my eyes, blinding me.

"Shine that light again. I thought I saw his eyes open."

I knew that voice. It was Niles Manner. I quickly shut my eyes and desperately tried to freeze my body.

"You're seeing things, Niles, that kid is out cold." The other man flashed the light on me for a couple of seconds and then turned it off

"Yeah, Bob, my age must be getting to me." Manner laughed. Bob? It must be Bob Powers, I thought.

My senses were now wide awake, and I was fully aware of my surroundings. I felt a combination of dirt and sand in my hand as I lay in the cold pit trying not to move.

"Yeah, Mr. Manner, it would take a miracle for that kid to wake up. If he's not sleeping from the drugs on that rag, he's certainly sleeping from the butt of your gun. You really whacked his head." It was Jason and he was laughing.

"It was just a natural instinct. Anyway, the kid deserved it."

"Yeah, imagine if he broke the story," Bob Powers wondered out loud.

"I don't want to think about it. But, our work isn't over. I found out he left a message on Shane O'Connell's machine. I was able to have it erased in time, but, by the tone of it, he may have talked to O'Connell before about this. So, Jason, after you take care of the kid, take care of O'Connell—and Haggerty, the guy from the beach. Now, I need a smoke. What about you, Bob?"

"Yeah, I'm with you." I heard the two men walk away. I didn't open my eyes, though, because I knew Jason was still standing above me.

"Kid, you're giving new meaning to the phrase 'meeting the sandman.'" I heard him pull a lever or something. I felt a spray of sand fall from above me and whip my face, almost knocking off my glasses. His comment now made perfect sense to me. I was lying in a pit that was about eight feet deep. I shielded the sand from my face with my hand and could see Jason was gone. He must've joined Manner and Powers, I thought. Instead, I was staring at a metal tube that was spewing out pounds of sand by the second. They were going to bury me alive.

I didn't have time to be frightened. I stood up and saw the sand had covered the pit to my ankles. I had to act fast. The long steel tube was angled, so it was above the middle of the pit. I moved to the side of the tube, so I wasn't facing the opening, and tried to grab it. I reached up as high as I could, and I was just a couple of inches away. There was no way I could jump up and grab the tube because the sand was getting deep, trapping me in one place.

"My belt," I blurted to myself. I pulled my belt off. The sand was getting deeper and deeper. I used one hand to lasso the belt around the long steel tube and the other to grab the other end. As I tried to grab the other end, it slipped out of my hand. The sand was halfway up my chest, and I knew I only had one more chance. I was able to get the belt around the steel hose. That was the easy part. Reaching the other part of my belt was the hard part. I stretched to a point where I almost broke in two, but I was able to grab the other half of my belt. I pulled my body up like I was doing pull-ups and worked my legs free. I hung above the pit until the sand was high enough for me to climb out. Then I jumped up and ran through the darkness up the dunes, thanking God I was alive.

I was now able to see what the steel hose was connected to—a Belltown beach truck. That made sense. Mr. Powers's brother ran the Belltown beaches in the summer. He was probably also on Manner's payroll. The trucks high beams were on, and they lit up Manner, Powers, and Jason, who were all smoking. Manner said something to Jason and pointed in the direction of the pit. Jason walked over and flashed the light on what he assumed was my grave. Suddenly he stopped, and turned back and headed toward my supposed grave site. He flashed the light on the beach, and I knew what he had seen. I had dropped my belt when I had run from the beach.

I saw him look from side to side, and my stomach was turning. As he turned to yell to Manner and Powers, his voice was blocked out by the cry of sirens. Manner and Powers jumped in the limo without waiting for Jason. Jason dropped the belt and ran down the beach into the dark.

I saw Shane jump out of his cruiser and race after him into the night. Manner's limousine barreled down the road followed by three screaming cruisers but was suddenly cut off by another limousine coming in his direction. He swerved off the road and landed on the beach, the limo trapped in sand. Two minutes later, I saw Shane come out of the darkness escorting Jason, who was handcuffed and had blood spilling from his nose. I was heading down to Shane when I saw Gina's truck pull up and Maria jump out of the passenger seat.

What is she doing here? I thought. I walked toward the crowd. The blue and white lights were swirling. Police radios were blaring but in all that confusion I could make out Maria, who was yelling at the top of her lungs, "Where is Orville?" she yelled at Jason. I wanted to yell to her, but I couldn't open my mouth. Shane repeated her question, "Where is Orville?" He went toward Jason who was now being held by two other police officers.

Manner yelled "Let's stay calm!"

Jason relaxed and grinned. He looked at Maria and said, "Orville who?"

Maria screamed, "No! No! No! I never got to tell him . . ."

"Tell me what?" I said softly from behind her.

Maria turned around and leaped up to me, "Orville, you're alive!" I caught her and hugged her. "Of course, I'm alive."

She hugged me for a minute, and all our emotions came out in that hug.

"What is it you have to tell me?" I whispered in her ear.

"I don't think I have to tell you now," she whispered and gave me a tender kiss on the cheek.

"Me, either." I laughed while holding her.

Gina ran up and joined us. All three of us were hugging each other. Shane and Ryan came over to us.

Ryan gave me a high five. "Orville, you're one of the gutsiest kids I know."

"And craziest." Shane frowned.

"I learned from the best." I smiled and Shane couldn't hold back the smile.

"Nice work, Ryan." I was beaming.

"Thanks, but next time you get in trouble, take a taxi." Ryan laughed.

"Ryan, whatever you do, don't say next time. That only fuels this kid's fire."

"Who me?" I played dumb and we all laughed.

"By the way, how'd you guys find me?" We walked toward Gina's truck.

Shane shook his head. "It's a good thing you have friends. I just got back from Jamaica, and I'm in town for ten minutes when I get two phone calls, one from Ryan. He told me all about Boston. The other from Gina and Maria."

"Yeah, I saw that man grab you, and I ran to the telephone booth when Gina pulled up in her truck." Maria was calming down a bit.

"And we followed you and called Shane on my CB. I told you that CB was good for something." Gina laughed.

"Thank God for you guys or I'd be in Manner's Garden!"

"Manner's Garden?" Shane squinted.

"Yeah, that's what he calls this place, 'cause I guess I wasn't the first person he tried to plant here."

Shane ran over to his car, "O'Connell here." The dispatch answered, "Yes, Detective."

"Yeah, you better call the chief and send him out here. I have a feeling it's going to be a long night."

"You got that right." I nodded.

An EMT bandaged my head while I drank a cup of coffee and watched the scene. I couldn't believe what I was seeing. It was straight out of a movie. Twenty minutes before I had been alone about to be buried alive by one of the most respected political figures in the state, and now he was handcuffed, sitting in the back of a police cruiser. Boy, talk about strange twists. The beach was covered with search teams and dogs who were sniffing every inch of Manner Park. I was still shaking a bit.

Maria gave me a kiss and a warm embrace before Shane told her and Gina they had to leave the crime scene. But not before Shane spoke to Gina about not using her computer the way she did, even if it was for a case. Shane let me stay because I was a prime witness, and he still had a few questions for me. When the EMT finished bandaging me up, I decided I wanted to get a little closer to the action. Shane was at the cruiser, grilling Manner, Powers, and Jason with questions.

"How many bodies are out there?"

"I want my lawyer!" Manner protested.

"You'll get him soon enough. Come on, Congressman, if you help us now, it will be to your benefit," Shane advised.

"This is ridiculous. I didn't do anything wrong. I was just showing these men my park. I'm one of the most respected men in the state. I demand you take these cuffs off!"

I walked closer to the cruiser till I was in view of Manner.

"This is the kid?" Manner looked at me as if he'd never seen me before. "Hey, you're just an overimaginative kid. They've got nothing against me except your word against mine!"

"Why you!!"

Shane ran over and pulled me away." Orville, stop it. Don' let him get to you. It's over for him," Shane whispered in my ear.

"Yeah, but what if he's right? What if it's his word against mine?" I was getting scared.

"Believe me, it's not," Shane whispered again.

Manner interrupted. "Detective, this is very touching but I want to go to the station, now. You've delayed me long enough."

"OK, Congressman." Shane was unnaturally polite. "So, you're telling me there are no bodies on the park grounds." He shot me a look that said maybe my story was suspect.

"That's right. It's just this boy's silly imagination." Manner smiled.

"Of course, he tends to dream up things. I hope he's not dreaming this up."

"Shane?" I protested in shock.

Shane turned around and winked at me, and then turned back to Manner. I knew he was up to something.

"Oh, Congressman, if you're telling the truth, this could be very embarrassing for the department."

"For all of you, I guarantee it." Manner said acidly.

"In fact, I think I'll call off the search in a minute. But, before we go to the station to clear this up, I want you to meet someone. I think it would speed up this process."

Shane unhooked his walkie-talkie from his belt.

"Jameson, are you there?"

"Jameson, over." A static reply.

"Could you bring our friend in now?"

A police cruiser rolled slowly up the road. As it approached, Shane said, "You know, I just got back from Jamaica."

"Really?" Manner frowned.

"Yes, unfortunately it wasn't a pleasure trip."

The cruiser door opened and Jameson escorted a tanned, elderly man out of the car. The man walked over to Manner. Manner's face turned white.

"I believe, Congressman, that you have met Andrew MacNichol." Manner put his head down.

"Niles, it's been a long time." MacNichol stared straight into the cruiser.

"Come on, take me to the station!" Manner shouted.

"Niles, you took the best years of my life, and you

also made me have to live with the fact that I was part of that poor young woman's murder. I still have nightmares about it. I try to forget about it, but it stays with me every night. I want you to know I will never forget, and my memory will be quite clear when I take the stand and point you out." I could hear the pain in MacNichol's voice.

A chorus of barks interrupted us, and we all turned our attention to the edge of the beach. There was chaos as lanterns bobbed in the night until they all came together as one great light.

The walkie-talkie crackled, "Detective O'Connell, are you there?"

"Yeah, O'Connell here."

"I think you better get down here."

"What's going on?" Shane asked.

"Found skeletal remains."

"OK. Be right there."

Shane turned to Jameson, "Get Officer Braga and take these men away."

The walkie-talkie then crackled again, "Detective O'Connell?"

"Yeah."

"Skeletal remains."

"I know, I just got the word."

"No, Detective. Skeletal remains for body number two."

"Number two?"

"Yes, sir. What?" The voice shouted to someone in the background and then yelled into the walkie-talkie,

"Check that, sir, skeletal remains found of bodies number three and four. Detective, you better get down here. This place is beginning to look like the Belltown Cemetery!"

"OK, OK." Shane growled, "Get them outta here. I can't look at them anymore."

Officer Jameson started the engine and pressed the engine into action. We all watched as the cruiser flew into the night. Shane ran toward the beach, and I was left alone with Andrew MacNichol.

"Orville Jacques." He put out his hand.

"Yes," I answered and reluctantly shook his hand.

"Andrew MacNichol. Detective O'Connell told me that you are friends with Mr. Michaels."

"Yes, I am." I suddenly thought of Will. How was he? Was he still alive? He had to know the truth before it was too late.

"He's a good man. I want you to believe me. I am sorry for all the pain I have caused him." MacNichol lowered his head.

"Are you?" I was skeptical.

"I live every night with the knowledge that my actions caused someone to die. That night I told Katherine to come with me, I really didn't think they were going to kill her." He stopped for a second. "Then again, maybe I did. I still don't know. All I know is that they had a gun pointed at my mother's head. I was young. I didn't know what to do. But, when Detective O'Connell found me in Jamaica, I was relieved. I can finally ease my conscience. Will Michaels wasn't the only person who lost in this thing. I'm not making excuses. I know I was a coward, and I have to live with that. But I also lost. I never got to say good-bye to my parents. I never got to go to their funerals, and I never got to show them any of their grandchildren. But, thanks to you and Detective O'Connell, I can finally face Mr. Michaels. I'm going to the hospital now. Do you want to come?"

As much as I did, I answered, "No, I think it would be best if you faced him on your own."

"You're right, Orville. You're absolutely right. He's lucky to have you as a friend." He patted me softly on the shoulder.

"No, I'm lucky to have him." I shook my head. "Could you tell him I'll be there first thing in the morning?" I knew Will was a fighter, and the fight would keep him living another day. And maybe longer.

"Certainly, son." He walked over to one of the officers and they both got into a cruiser and drove off. Andrew MacNichol would soon be free of the past ...

CHAPTER
TEN

Wɪᴛʜ ᴇᴀᴄʜ ʙᴀʀᴋ of a dog, it seemed another grave was found. In an hour, eight had been found. All the graves bordered the park and the edge of the beach. I was more than lucky to be alive, I thought as I watched a man and two women brushing sand and dirt off a skeleton, the way archaeologists do when finding dinosaur bones. My stomach turned.

"I know, pretty sick, isn't it?" Shane stood beside me.

I shook my head in disgust.

"Yeah, there are some sick people in this world. And it's a strange feeling you get when you catch one."

"What do you mean?" I asked.

"Well, you're relieved you caught them, but you say

to yourself,'Why did it go this far?'" Shane paused. "Now, I called your parents."

"And?" I rolled my eyes.

"Well, let's just say they're not too pleased you played cops and robbers again." Shane gave me a smirk.

"Yeah, I can imagine. Is my dad coming to pick me up?"

"No, I'll drive you, and you can fill me in on your little adventure." He pulled out his tape recorder.

"OK, but first I've got one question of my own."

"Shoot." Shane smiled.

"How did you find Andrew MacNichol?"

"Well, remember that file you stole off my desk?"

"I didn't take it. I was going to but . . ."

"C'mon Orville, you would've needed some of that info to get into that much trouble." Shane folded his arms.

"OK, but I didn't steal it. I borrowed it."

"I'll take care of that later. Well, anyway, Orville, you overlooked the personal profile of Andrew MacNichol."

"What would that serve?" I quizzed.

"It stated that Andrew MacNichol was an expert diver."

"Yeah." I was dying to hear him continue.

"Well, I put that in the back of my mind when I asked around town if anyone had seen him."

I could tell Shane was proud of his work.

"And?"

"And, one person told me that he could've sworn he saw MacNichol in Jamaica years ago when he was on vacation."

He waited for my response.

"Then what?"

"So, I figured if it was MacNichol, he might still be into diving. Maybe he owned his own dive shop or something. So, I called my friend at the FBI, and we began a search. He paused. "Now it's your turn."

"Well," I paused and was interrupted by an officer running up to Shane carrying a plastic bag.

"Detective, I think you better take a look."

"Yes, Warner, what is it?" Shane took the plastic bag.

"It's a driver's license. It was buried with one of the bodies."

Officer Warner gave the flashlight to Shane who shined it on the faded driver's license. Shane read it out loud, "The Commonwealth of Massachusetts, Pervis, Jack, 9 Mayflower Court, Belltown."

Shane saw me lower my head, "I'm still new to this town. Does the name Jack Pervis mean anything to you, Orville?"

"It means everything, Shane. It means everything."

I jumped on my mountain bike at 8:45 AM I was still a little groggy considering I hardly got a wink of sleep the night before. I had told my parents everything, and yes, they were a little upset, to say the least. They were proud of my tenacity, but they were also upset that I didn't use my head while searching for the truth. They were right. I never considered the danger. My parents were also ticked off about my skipping school. I would have to do extra chores for that. Shane also penalized me. For the next three Saturdays, I'd have to paint his office because I took the Katherine Stinson files. But now I knew the truth, and that's all that really mattered.

I told Shane almost everything I had found out, except for one point. I knew if I told him, it could become police evidence, and I felt there was still some unfinished business in the case.

I clutched the key in my jacket pocket as I walked into Belltown Bank & Trust at exactly 9:00 AM. The bank was just opening, and it was very quiet. In fact, the entire town was quiet. I knew after Shane's 12:30 press conference, the whole town would be buzzing. But, for now, the events on the beach were still a secret.

I presented the key, and Mr. Adams, the bank president, showed me down a hallway and unlocked a room filled with metal boxes. Each box was numbered in order. We walked down three rows and there it was—127. Mr. Adams unlocked the case and held the box, and I took it from him.

"All right, Orville, if you will just follow me."

We went over to another room and he unlocked the door. There was a chair and table in the room.

"You can unlock your box in this room. When you're done, just press this button, and then I will unlock the door." Mr. Adams said.

"Thank you, Mr. Adams." I smiled.

Mr. Adams shut the door, and I sat down and put the box on the table. I took a deep breath and unlocked the box. There was a stack of papers, and I picked up the first one and read it: "This is a safe deposit box reserved by FBI agent Lawrence Thames for the children or loved ones of Katherine Stinson. This box contains documents that explain Ms. Stinson's past, so her children or loved ones will be able to understand why and what she did."

That's why the box is paid up for a hundred years, I thought. Margaret Ann Campbell *a.k.a.* Katherine Stinson wanted her loved ones or children to know the truth, but not until much later in life when their own safety was guaranteed. I shuffled through papers and birth certificates and came to an article from the *Chicago Tribune.* The headline: "Daughter of Murder Victims Testifies." I put it aside. I knew what it would contain. Under those papers was a picture. I shivered when I saw it. It was a picture of a woman I had never seen before, but I knew her. I read the back of the photo— Margaret Ann Campbell/Katherine Stinson.

I put the picture aside, and then my eyes popped out of my head. I was looking at a computer disk. "How did a computer disk get in the box? There were no computers back in the forties," I thought out loud.

It read, "N.M. by J.P. 6/8/87."

Then it dawned on me. Niles Manner by Jack Pervis, June 8, 1987. It was the article that Jack Pervis had written exposing Niles Manner's past. After he found the key and the truth, he probably decided to hide his article in the box for safekeeping.

There was one other thing in the bottom of the box, which would finally close the door on the past: a sealed envelope addressed to Will Michaels. I gathered everything into my backpack and then pushed the button three times.

I flew on my mountain bike to Belltown Hospital. I knew the letter would tell Will not only the truth but that Katherine's love would never die. Maybe, the letter would lift his spirits to a level where he would get better.

I also thought of Jack Pervis. He was similar to Will and Andrew MacNichol. Rumors had haunted his name—people said that he was a drug runner. In actuality he was a hero. He broke the story back in 1987, long before Shane and me, but was killed before he could get it printed. He died trying to find the truth. In that box there was a clear sign that told me he wasn't out just for a story like a sleazy investigative reporter. The letter to Will was sealed. Pervis never opened it. I admired him for that. He was a class act. I knew what I had to do with the computer disk.

I wanted to hold my breath and close my eyes and make a wish when I walked into Will's room. I wished to see him propped up in his bed, cracking jokes with the nurses. Reality punched me in the heart. I slowly walked up to his bed and looked down at him. I thought he was sleeping, but his eyes were open.

"Orv . . . ille." He forced a weak smile.

"Will." Just looking at him my voice was cracking.

"You . . . did . . . well, son." Will's eyes were teary.

"Thanks, I wanted you to know the truth. I didn't want you to ever have to ask why again. Did Mr. MacNichol see you?" I eased closer.

"Yes. I hated him for years . . . and now I realize . . . he was just as much a victim . . . I was just like the town . . . I believed what I wanted to . . . I'm sorry for that. We made peace."

"Will, this is addressed to you." I handed the sealed letter to Will, and he slowly sat up a little.

"Could . . ." he coughed, "you open it . . . Orville?"

"Sure." I opened it and handed it to him.

He read the letter and his eyes watered more. After a few minutes, he handed it back to me and said, "Katherine wrote that in case she ever . . . were . . . to leave me. She said if she did leave it would only be out of love. She didn't . . . want me to get hurt . . . She . . . always thought of . . . other . . . people . . . never herself." He handed me the letter and slumped down into the bed.

"Orville . . . you've given me a gift . . . no one could . . ." Will was fading off.

"Will." I was getting nervous.

You've given me . . . peace . . . of . . . mind. I'm going . . . to miss . . . you."

"Will! Don't talk that way!" I yelled at him.

"You're like . . . a son . . . " Will ignored my yell.

"Will, stop talking like that! It's not the end."

"Orville . . . I'm dying . . . It's OK." His voice was soft.

"No, it's not OK." My eyes were burning and I couldn't hold back. "Will, you can't die. You can't die! We just found out the truth! You can't die!" I gave into all my emotions. It was really happening. He was giving up the fight.

"Orville . . . son . . . you see . . . now I can die . . . Someday you'll . . . understand." His eyes were almost closed.

I handed him the picture of Katherine. He stared at it for a few seconds with his eyes hardly open.

A smile came across his face, "Could . . ." he coughed hard, "you . . . put . . . on . . . the record?" He slowly pointed to the record player, and I nodded. I knew which record he meant. I put it on and Frank Sinatra's voice warmed the room. Will's smile was alive. He was back in 1946 dancing with Katherine Stinson.

I'll never smile again until I smile at you.
I'll never laugh again, what good would it do?
I'll never love again, I'm so in love with you.

When the song ended, all I could hear was the needle on the record indicating the song was over, and the sound of my own sobs as I held my friend's hand for the last time.

The sun was just waking up as I carried the small brown box in my hand. There was a chill in the air, but it was a good chill, the type that makes you feel alive. I came to the jetties and walked out as far as I could go and sat down and looked out at the Atlantic Ocean. Waves jumped onto the jetties and splashed me a bit. I didn't move. I absorbed the spray, tasting the salty air while wiping away my saltier tears.

I was trying to make sense of everything. I thought if *I* could solve the case somehow that would save Will. I still had a lot of growing up to do. My first step was to do what Will had asked of me in a letter. I took it out and read it again.

> Dear Orville,
>
> I just want to thank you for being the best friend a man could ask for. You are like a son to me. Tonight Mr. MacNichol met me and told me what you did. You risked your life to save my conscience. I am forever grateful. If I get any power in the next life, I will always look out for you. God has given you a great gift—the ability to find out the truth. I hope you never lose that gift. I do have to ask you one last favor. Could you please scatter my ashes off the jetties at Cranberry Beach? That way, I can join my true love for one more dance. Someday, you will understand the value of the gift you have given me.
>
> With love, your friend,
> Will Michaels

I folded the note and put it back in my pocket. My vision was blurred as I opened the box and let the wind take the ashes and cast them into the sea.

"Goodbye, my friend," I managed between sobs, and suddenly I had a strange feeling. I was filled with joy. I was beginning to understand the gift. He could join Katherine with a clear conscience. She broke up with him out of love.

And now they were back together, and Niles Manner couldn't touch that love. He couldn't hurt it. Their love would live forever. I smiled as I watched two seagulls swoop down over the ocean, and I remembered what Mr. Haggerty said about Cranberry Beach. It was peaceful. It was like being with God. As I walked along the beach, I thought of the gifts Will had given me, and I knew somewhere in heaven "I'll never Smile Again" was playing andtwo voices were one, and they were *finally* smiling again . . .

EPILOGUE

THE BELLTOWN BANK & Trust was buzzing. Coffee was being poured by the gallons at Coffee Obsession. The old locals at Bill's Donuts were shaking their heads in disbelief. Everyone was talking about it—the biggest news story of the year in Massachusetts. Everyone knew retired Congressman Niles Manner was in police custody, but no one knew why until the *Cape Cod Times* broke a story that the *Boston Globe,* the *Boston Herald,* and all the Boston TV stations couldn't get a handle on. A case that was cracked years before and was just coming out. The front page read:

New Evidence Links Congressman to Murder

By Jack Pervis June 8, 1987

Looking at the headline, I smiled to myself. Jack Pervis was finally getting his by-line for breaking the biggest story in Belltown history.

About the Author

T. M. Murphy lives in Falmouth, Massachusetts. When he is not writing or cheering for the Boston Red Sox, Mr. Murphy enjoys teaching creative writing to young people. He lives and teaches his Just Write It class in a converted garage he calls The Shack.

Photo by Amy Hamilton